SHADOWS IN THE STARS

SHADOWS IN THE STARS
BOOK 1

T.W.M. ASHFORD

Copyright © 2024 by T.W.M. Ashford
All rights reserved.

No part of this book may be reproduced in any form or by any electronic or mechanical means, including information storage and retrieval systems, without written permission from the author, except for the use of brief quotations in a book review.

Any characters in this publication are fictitious and any resemblance to real persons, living or dead, is purely coincidental.

Cover design by Tom Ashford

DARK STAR PANORAMA

Dark Star Panorama is the shared universe of sci-fi stories in which *Shadows in the Stars* takes place. Other series include *Final Dawn, Kapamentis Crime* and *War for New Terra*.

To hear about new releases and receive exclusive free content, sign up for T.W.M. Ashford's mailing list at the website below.

www.twmashford.com

BOOKS IN THE "DARK STAR PANORAMA" UNIVERSE

Final Dawn Series

- The Final Dawn
- Thief of Stars
- A Dark Horizon
- The New World
- The Tin Soldiers
- Ghost of the Father
- The Stellar Abyss
- The Edge of Night
- The Fatal Dark

War for New Terra Series

- Sigma
- Iron Nest
- Royal Blood

Shadows in the Stars Series

- Shadows in the Stars
- Shadows in the Snow

Kapamentis Crime Series

- A Cut Below
- Cut to the Bone
- Cut and Shut
- The Final Cut

Standalone Novels

- Saturnalia

SELECT NON-DSP TITLES

- Checking Out (Box Set)
- Blackwater (Box Set)
- The Portrait Lingers Like a Whisper
- Gerald Oddman

SHADOWS IN THE STARS

CHAPTER ONE

The flames of wax candles flickered like snake tongues in the damp gloom. Short-lived shadows stalked across rough walls of crag and rock. Somewhere deep in the subterranean labyrinth, a stalactite dripped lazily into a murky pool.

Hooded figures shuffled through the darkness.

They chanted together, slow and deep in their throats, pairing ominous harmonies. Their long, desert-brown robes draped behind them, brushing tracks through the dust on the tunnel floor. Their hands were clasped together in prayer beneath their pendulous sleeves.

A six-legged lizard jerked its head up as it heard their order coming, then slithered away through a crack in the nearest boulder.

Into a grand chamber they poured, a stream of monks marching two abreast. Ancient statues carved from red rock stood around the edge of the cavern, each a dozen metres tall. The procession circled the floor counter-clockwise, spiralling slowly inwards like a ruptured starship tumbling towards a black hole, until the last two monks entered and the chamber was full. Their throaty chant ceased instantly. The only sound remaining was that of large braziers crackling.

Precisely in the centre of the chamber was a huge gemstone.

It was the size and shape of an ostrich egg, one whose shell sparkled as if it were cut from a giant diamond. The flames of the braziers kissed its sharp, uneven surface. Their amber light was reflected across the stoic faces of its captivated audience in sparkling, shimmering waves.

Their collective attention remained on the ovoid jewel even as the final member appeared in the alcove high above them. This was the High Priest, the most senior amongst their order, and he alone was hoodless. His skin was the colour of desert sand. His leathery, white-wisped head was host to a thick beard of fleshy tendrils. Clasped in his wrinkled hand was an ornate golden sceptre topped with an equally golden medallion. A beast resembling a wyvern adorned its face.

He spread his arms wide, holding the sceptre aloft as if it were a spear, and spoke in a surprisingly fierce voice for his years. The words followed a dark, drawn-out rhythm. They belonged to a language long extinct. But everybody present knew what the words signified, even if nobody could translate them directly anymore.

Collectively, they were the Rites of Skinesh.

They were *tradition* – one carried out by generation after generation since time immemorial.

The High Priest finished his speech, then nodded.

"Proceed," he announced in his local tongue.

Two of the hooded monks stepped forward from the silent spiral and, grabbing the long wooden handles of the silky stretcher on which the jewel rested, lifted the priceless artefact off the rocky floor. The rest closed ranks, and together they carefully marched out of the chamber through another ancient lava tunnel. Satisfied with proceedings, the High Priest turned and vanished from his alcove.

Again their order chanted, their haunted voices carried alongside the egg down rock tube after rock tube, until eventually the dim candlelight died and their lungs tasted cleaner air...

A stage outside the hypogean temple. Wooden boards neatly arranged under the shadow of a crooked outcrop supported by eight chestnut-coloured pillars. Beyond the stage, hundreds – perhaps thousands – more believers watched and waited under the myriad stars. Midnight waves could be heard crashing and retreating over the nearby shore.

The monks spread out to fill the rear of the stage – all except the two carrying the artefact, who continued onward to a lonely plinth set in the stage's centre. It was at this time that the High Priest joined them, eliciting a hushed shiver of excitement through the patient crowd.

"Friends, family, citizens of Keet," he announced in a voice far more creaky than that in which he'd performed the sacred rites. "Thank you for gathering here tonight. For two weeks we have mourned the loss of our blessed krustallos. For two weeks we have fasted, as the scripture dictates. And all the while, the Purple Sunset continues to consume."

A general murmur rippled through the audience. Many raised their heads to the heavens. Even in the late evening, a dark, foreboding bruise in the sky could be seen blocking out a stretch of stars.

"Yet we must not fret," he continued, raising a wrinkled

palm for quiet. "Our Great Protector may have departed this world, but from death, life may begin anew."

He stepped aside. The two monks set down the stretcher and delicately transferred the jewel to the cushioned plinth. The crowd held its collective breath. Once set, the High Priest removed the medallion from the top of his sceptre and, with his back to his audience, activated the plinth's locking mechanism. Four clamps contracted and secured the twinkling egg in position.

The High Priest carefully reattached the medallion to his sceptre before spinning around with his arms raised and a radiant smile spread across his face.

"The Cradle of the Krustallos is set. Let the Sunrise Celebrations begin!"

The crowd erupted in rapturous cheers and applause. Lights bloomed all across the city, dispelling the darkness. Oil lanterns, strings of fairy lights, neon signs on store fronts. Somebody even released a swarm of fireflies into the dusky sky. Musical groups launched into lively performances; steel drums fought to be heard over the screech of electronic synths. Grills were lit. Saloons handed out free drinks. Citizens danced and embraced in the streets. Even a few of the younger acolytes were tempted into throwing back their hoods and joining the revelry.

High Priest Szaladar watched his neighbours party with great fondness. He knew many of them by name. The parties, the pageantry. After the miserable fortnight through which they'd just suffered, the people of Keet needed this.

He turned back to the jewel and ran a gentle hand over its crystalline exterior, imagining he could feel a warmth within. The egg was close to hatching. Two weeks was all it took. It would be the only egg to hatch in his lifetime. A krustallos lived for centuries. He was lucky to officiate a Sunrise ceremony at all.

Somebody let off a firework above the temple. Szaladar jumped, alarmed, then laughed as he watched the shower of yellow sparks descend over the city.

Finally, he thought, all was good on the quiet planet of Nasako once more.

CHAPTER TWO

Sheni Dupont slammed his fist down on the chipped wooden table, grinned heartily, and asked, "Another round, Gecki?"

"We can't afford it."

"That wasn't the question. Do you want one?"

The reptilian lounging in the chair opposite him scratched her scaly cheek with a long, black claw, and shrugged.

"Yeah, screw it. Put it on the tab."

Sheni clicked his fingers in triumph, pushed back his chair and rose unsteadily to his feet. He wasn't drunk yet. Nowhere near, in fact. They didn't have the credits for *that*. It was just that the floor of the bar was so damn uneven...

Still the best port in the galaxy by a country parsec, though.

The Corpse & Casket was a one-stop shop for pirates, thieves and raiders alike. Presently in a lazy orbit around the Baratarian star, the station offered a place to dock and refuel one's ship, louse-infested accommodation for desperate hitchhikers, dubious avenues for offloading particularly 'hot' cargo – and, of course, the titular watering hole. The beers weren't all that great, but they were cheap and they never stopped flowing.

Like many of the regulars, Sheni lived aboard his ship. But even with the *Silver Hart* docked only a couple of hundred metres from where he presently stood, the Corpse & Casket felt like a home away from home.

He jerked his head back just in time to dodge a glass bottle being lobbed across the room.

Not that he'd ever let any of these reprobates into his *actual* house, of course, should he ever find himself able to afford one...

The Corpse & Casket welcomed all sorts. Literally. The galaxy was occupied by thousands of alien species of varying intelligence, and practically all of them had less desirable denizens who visited the port from time to time. As a humanoid – let alone an actual *human* – Sheni was hilariously outnumbered. Diminutive Scrap Rats yapped and scratched themselves in the corners. Hulking rhinoceros creatures called Alpha Rhoden put enormous pressure on creaking chairs already on the cusp of becoming firewood. An eight armed cephalopod played a dangerous knife game with a cyber-augmented insectoid. A pair of red-horned beasts with black, leathery wings hung upside-down from the rafters, tittering and sucking at blood-packs.

There was no denying the fact that most of the bar's patrons were cutthroats and murderers. Even those in possession of a few moral principles weren't afraid to disable a starship's thrusters and render its crew stranded in the cold void if it meant lining their pockets with a few credits. Sheni didn't consider himself remotely in the same league as them. His crew of small-time spacers simply didn't fit in anywhere else.

Hell, half the lunatics present would probably kill him and Gecki if they thought they'd be any profit in it. Not inside the Corpse & Casket, though. Even a pirate bar has rules.

Sheni reached the bar having navigated an overturned chair and a puddle of vomit. Overhead, neon signs for various beverage brands flickered on and off beside the mounted head of a Queflian sand shark. Hundreds of flasks, vials and bottles suitable for dozens of different metabolisms lined the ramshackle shelves behind. Seven drunken fools sat with various degrees of success along the counter. He squeezed between two comatose regulars he assumed still drew breath.

"Hey, Copper John. Two beers, yeah?"

The bartender squeaked and wheezed down the counter towards him. Copper John was an automata, a sentient robot who'd killed his old master and gone on the run a few decades prior. His four long arms full of gears and pistons made pouring drinks a breeze. His brass head was devoid of facial features, and he wore a necklace of teeth and playing cards to differentiate himself from the taps and pipes. Newer visitors sometimes assumed he was a pushover on account of being a synthetic, but Copper John had been known to shoot troublemakers with the shotgun he kept stashed behind the barrels. Nobody could remember who originally built the station, but if anyone could be said to own the Corpse & Casket, it was him.

"Two beers?" he replied in a voice like a fax machine. "You still haven't paid for your last two yet. Last two hundred, more like."

"Come on, John." Sheni reached over the counter and

punched the automata lightly on the metal shoulder. "It all goes on the tab, doesn't it?"

"A tab isn't a high score, Sheni. You have to pay it off eventually."

"And I will. Eventually. You know we're good for it."

Commotion broke out at the other end of the room. Copper John extended his mechanical neck for a better look. One of the elephantine Alpha Rhoden had stood up from her table and was dangling a small green alien above it by one of its spindly legs.

"Somebody had better take responsibility for this jelly bean before I pin it to the bloody wall," she grumbled.

Sheni groaned.

"Stop unscrewing the table bolts, Alan," he shouted from the bar, "and go sit next to Gecki."

The Alpha Rhoden dropped the olive green creature onto the table, sending empty beer bottles and burnt-out cigarette butts cascading onto the wooden floor. Sheni winced. Alan leapt down and hurried across the crowded room to Gecki, a dopey smile plastered across his green face. The alien was only a couple of feet tall and shaped like a melon that someone had squished at the sides. A pair of large eyes bulging out from the top of his torso stared in opposite directions to one another. Nobody knew what species Alan belonged to, or even what his real name was. The gibbering idiot had been on the *Silver Hart* back when Gecki stole it, and he'd been an inseparable part of the crew ever since.

Sheni shook his head in exasperation.

"Better make that three beers," he said to Copper John, flashing an apologetic smile.

"Two beers and a mudberry juice," the cantankerous automata replied, "coming right up..."

The white-haired patron closest to Sheni shivered out of his drunken stupor. All of the humanoid's limbs had been hacked off and replaced with robotic prosthetics over the years. One of his eyes was a cybernetic camera lens, and the other was a black eight-ball that rolled around in its socket uncontrollably. The pensioner tried disembarking his stool and almost toppled over backwards.

"Woah there, Old Guntho." Sheni helped him down. "Careful. I think somebody needs to go sleep this one off, eh?"

"Thank you, young man," the ancient pirate croaked. *Young man?* Sheni was a shade past forty. "Most raiders these days – they ain't got no respect for their elders, you know?"

"I hear you," Sheni said kindly as he aimed Old Guntho towards the door. The decrepit cyborg was a regular at the Corpse & Casket. Surely he had to sleep *somewhere* besides the bar. "You got a room at Peggi's?"

The leathery pirate gave Sheni a mechanical thumbs-up and tottered out of the bar. Sheni thanked Copper John for the drinks and carried them back to Gecki's table. Alan sipped his juice through a metal straw pocked with rust. He seemed to enjoy it. It was hard to tell sometimes, what with the little weirdo only having the one facial expression.

"Okay, Gecki." Sheni pointed his mug at her. "Now that I've got a fresh drink in my hand, tell me – how broke are we, exactly?"

"We were broke before. Now we're the bits and pieces dumped in the trash."

Alan may have been forever grinning, but Gecki had a frown chiseled into a face of cold granite. She was a six-foot-eight bipedal reptilian – a Eureptix, to be precise – capable of tearing off a man's arm with a single tug. Her currently mint-green scales could shift colour and render her almost invisible and, unlike most of her victims, she could regrow lost limbs. Her species had practically evolved to be thieves. Sheni was keenly aware that her frosty demeanour was the primary reason why the other pirates at the Corpse & Casket refrained from picking fights with him. That, and he wasn't afraid to get a round in. She was nearly blind in her left eye, which had lost its yellow colour and turned a cloudy grey.

Even with a translator chip planted in the back of his neck, Sheni couldn't pronounce her true Eureptix name. He wasn't born with the right combination of vocal chords and pheromone glands. Gecki was the closest most species could manage without drenching the angry lizard in phlegm.

"So we've got no credits left at all, is that what you're saying? Even the emergency stash is empty?"

"It's been empty for half a cycle now, you idiot. You wasted the last of it gambling on the holo-races."

"Hey." Sheni looked down into his mug as he drank. "Those races were meant to be rigged..."

"Yes, against you! And only the gods know how we're gonna clear the debt we incurred paying off the bookies..."

"Ah, stop worrying about everything so much." Sheni leaned back and put his boot up on the table. "We'll figure something out. We always do."

Gecki hissed something derogatory under her breath, which Sheni chose to ignore. The lizard needed to loosen up. That's why they'd come all the way out to the Baratarian system, wasn't it? To escape the up-tight rules and regulations of the wider Ministerium, not fret about petty loan sharks.

"Did I hear you're in need of some quick credits?" asked a sheepish voice behind their backs.

Sheni and Gecki groaned in unison. Alan gurgled contentedly.

"What do you want, Two-Toe Tim?" Sheni glanced over his shoulder. "I swear, this had better not be another of your get-rich-quick schemes..."

The short man standing behind him smelled of stale beer and moth balls. He was dressed in standard raider rags and a leather vest-jacket not dissimilar to Sheni's own. His small, mousey demeanour gave people the impression he might accidentally slip through the cracks in the planks beneath his well-worn boots.

"Hey, don't be like that, guys." Two-Toe Tim looked between them uneasily. "Us humans have got to stick together. Ain't that right, Sheni?"

He wasn't wrong. Ever since the evacuation of Earth, Homo sapiens had practically become an endangered species. Two-Toe Tim was certainly the only other human pirate Sheni had come across over the years. Most of their kind were quite content to settle down in the colonies on New Terra.

"How come you've only got two toes, anyway?" Gecki rasped. "Frostbite get them, or something?"

"I haven't got two toes," Tim sighed despondently. "I'm *missing* two toes. You know, from the usual ten. Usual for a human, I mean," he hurriedly added, sweating under the heat of Gecki's glare. "Lost them in a shipyard accident, if you must know. Dropped a skip drive on them. And it's just Tim, by the way. Tim is absolutely fine."

"Come on then, Two-Toes," Sheni said. "Out with it. What's this harebrained idea of yours?"

Tim hesitated for a moment, then hurried around to the

other side of the table and sat down hard on the one remaining chair.

"Have either of you heard of the planet Nasako?" he asked.

"No," Sheni replied.

"Yes," Gecki responded, glancing at her crewmate. "Small rock out in the Morg system. Not a place where much happens."

"Exactly," Two-Toe Tim said enthusiastically. "Which is why it's the perfect place for a score. Minimal Ministerium oversight, you know? And the locals are piss-poor. Barely any municipal security to worry about."

"It'll take a quarter-tank of fuel to get to Nasako." Gecki crossed her arms. "There's plenty worth stealing that's a lot closer. This target of yours must be pretty valuable."

"Oh, it is." Tim leaned across the table conspiratorially. "We're talking about an egg made entirely of taaffeite crystal."

Gecki reared her head back and hissed.

"Oh, gods. Not another egg. Botching that Chiboraan job almost got us killed."

"It's not a *real* egg," Tim insisted. "Least, I don't think it is. Just a really ornate one used for ceremonies. You know, like a Fabergé Egg," he said to Sheni. "Remember them?"

"Course I do," Sheni replied, his interest piqued. "Russian jewellery made for the Imperial family, right? Emperor-level stuff. Insanely valuable," he added for Gecki's benefit.

"Taaffeite crystal does fetch a high price on the black market," Gecki mused. "And this thing's easy to grab, you say?"

"Displayed outside for anyone to take," Tim replied. "It's part of some ceremony that takes place every couple hundred years, or whatever. Just a few local guards on watch, nothing you can't handle. Like you said, it's a backwater planet. The Nasakoans are a very trusting people."

"So why do you need us?" Sheni asked. "Why not go grab it yourself?"

"Don't have a ship, do I? Been stuck on this blasted station for weeks now. So, what do you say? Fifty-fifty split?"

"You're having a laugh, aren't you?" Sheni snorted. "All you've done is pass on what you heard from someone else."

"Finder's fee, ain't it? Three ways, then. Thirty-three point three percent each."

"We have four crew members," Gecki snapped, jabbing a claw at Alan. "Counting this green goon and our pilot."

Alan reached the end of his juice and made a slurping sound with his straw that continued until Gecki pulled it from his mouth.

"Fine," Tim said through gritted teeth. "An even split of the profits between everyone on board, and you let me join your team."

Sheni almost spat out his drink.

"No freaking way." Gecki laughed. "We're barely keeping ourselves afloat as it is. There's no space for anyone else on the *Silver Hart,* not even with this take of yours."

"Presuming the rumours you've heard are true," Sheni added.

"Exactly." Gecki leaned back and picked at her teeth with a claw. "We'd be taking all the risk. Eighty-five to fifteen percent split in our favour, and we drop you off wherever you want after we're done. Final offer."

They waited patiently while Tim's jaw clenched and his eyes flickered between the two of them. Sheni suspected he cared more about being assigned to a permanent crew than what his share of the credits would be.

"Don't want this score? Fine." Two-Toe Tim suddenly stood up with his hands raised in defeat. "I'll take it to Thunderskull instead. I just thought I'd give a fellow human first dibs."

"Woah, now." Sheni pulled Tim back down. "Steady on, man. Is your head screwed on tight? Thunderskull's madder than a Krettelian in a cage. You don't want to get mixed up with him."

"You think I want to get mixed up with *anyone* here?" Tim hissed quietly. "That's why I came to you first. Thunderhead's no worse than the rest of these guys, is he?"

"You want a bet? Only last week, he spaced a guy for getting lost on his way back from shore leave. Could have just marooned his sorry ass, but no – Thunderskull waited until the engineer was back on board and then shoved him out the airlock once they reached orbit. The guy's a murderous psychopath, man."

"So? *You've* both killed people."

"He's right," Gecki said with a lethargic shrug.

"No, he's not!"

"What do you call blowing up all those Prymalis attack ships, then?"

"We were defending Kapamentis against an invading force. Billions of lives were at stake. We're practically war heroes!"

"And Copperhead and his crew? Was that a noble battle, too?"

"No, but he was planning to torture our friends. Maniac, just like Thunderskull. It's all in the name, you know. He had it coming." He dismissed the argument and turned back to Two-Toe Tim, who was grimacing. "It doesn't matter. The point is, we don't make a habit of hurting people. And we certainly don't enjoy it."

"Sometimes I do," Gecki added, cracking a rare smile.

"Whatever, guys." Tim rose from his chair again with a tired sigh. "If you don't wanna work with me, someone else will. Just don't expect me to buy you a round when I'm rolling in credits."

"Good luck," said Sheni, tipping his mug in Tim's direction. He disappeared back into the throng, weaving between boisterous tables, already making a beeline for another potential business partner.

"Idiot's gonna get himself killed," Gecki said, throwing back the rest of her beer.

"Ah, he'll be all right." Ever the optimist, Sheni swatted the idea away. "Somebody in here'll bite."

"Yeah. Literally."

Gecki pulled a pocket watch-shaped comm-link from her jacket. She had a notification from Xotl, their pilot. Time to head back to the ship.

"You finished?" she rasped, standing up.

"Yeah, mug's empty," Sheni replied, tipping it upside down. "Not that I got to enjoy it much, you know? Bloody Two-Toes. Honestly," he added as somebody behind him broke a chair over another patron's head. "You come to the Corpse & Casket, you expect a bit of peace and quiet."

CHAPTER
THREE

The concourse of the Corpse & Casket space station was only marginally less rowdy than its titular bar. Black Rock Raiders wearing tarnished metal gauntlets and greaves guzzled ale and sang out of key. Spacers wheeled stacks of crates containing protein tins and counterfeit sims out from the docks. Ad hoc stalls assembled from pylons and strips of raggedy tent fabric sold rifles, prescription meds and prototype tech implants. Aliens of ill repute waved hands and tentacles from corrugated balconies. Somebody was frying noodles; Sheni could smell the steam. The rest of the air tasted dry and recycled from the barely functioning atmospheric processors and was filled with the sound of mechanics hard at work.

They passed Old Guntho only a few metres down from the entrance to the bar, out cold on a bed of frozen eels. He was a staple of the station, so nobody paid him any attention. Sheni considered waking him, then wondered what the point would be. He'd only black out again further down the hall. Better to let him sleep it off.

A smiling, feather-templed Kerulian sauntered out of

the front door of the boarding house as they marched past it towards the docks.

"Gecki. Sheni. You got any goodies for me?"

Peggi Slim was both the proprietor of the Rusty Bucket boarding house and the port's resident fence, which meant she bought anything stolen or illegal stashed in people's cargo holds and then flipped it on the black market. Gecki gave her a curt, upward nod of recognition. Sheni wrapped his arm around her shoulders and squeezed.

"Not this time, Peggi. Going through a bit of a tough spell."

"Yeah, you ain't alone there. Loadsa crews having trouble scoring big since the major empires started pumping credits back into the Ministerium's coffers. Business'll pick back up, though."

"And you know where we'll come when it does," Sheni said with a wink as he walked away.

"Possessory obfuscation," Alan gurgled, smiling up at Peggi gormlessly.

"Good to see you, too, little fella," she said, rubbing the top of his smooth, lime green head. "Go on, now. You don't wanna lose your friends."

Alan waddled after them. Gecki had received another blinking notification on her tiny, pocket-size comm-link. Sheni noticed the message was from Xotl. Their pilot tried opening a channel with them a second later.

"Someone's persistent," she said, rolling her one yellow eye as she accepted his call. "Yes, Xotl. We're on our way back. Stop fretting."

A small blue hologram beamed up from the disc in Gecki's hand. It displayed a rather distressed starfish standing upright on two of its five thick arms. It didn't possess any facial features besides the beak-like mouth in the centre of its body, but after years spent travelling the cosmos together, Sheni could pick up on their subtle visual tells. The Xocha's suckers were more dilated than usual.

"You need to get down here right now," Xotl said in a spluttering voice like a brick hitting soft butter. "We have company."

"Course we do, man!" Sheni beamed goofily over Gecki's shoulder. "It's a busy station!"

"No, you fool," Xotl replied. "It's Morty Slugbarrow. He's threatening to clamp the ship."

"What's that slimeball doing on the station?" Gecki snarled at the hologram as they passed under the arches of Dock B-3. "Get out there and stop him!"

"You know I can't do that."

"Gah! Fine." She broke into a sprint down a connecting corridor full of brass pipes and looping wires. Sheni struggled to keep up. "Just keep him distracted, then. Maybe if we can sneak on board without him—"

"Going somewhere, Gecki?"

Slugbarrow was waiting for them at the entrance to the hangar. The loan shark had the head of a tapir and the short, stocky body of a carnival strongman. A pot belly protruded from his natty, brown undershirt. His floppy snout was purple and engorged from decades of drinking. To either side of it sat a pair of beady, hungry eyes.

Sheni stiffened. Two of the lackeys flanking Slugbarrow wielded plasma rifles. This wasn't a social call, nor a fight they could win.

"Slugbarrow," Gecki rasped in a voice like two sheets of sandpaper rubbed together. "We were just on our way to see you..."

"Were you now? How convenient." Slugbarrow smiled, his plump lips parting to reveal two rows of chipped, yellowing molars. "I assume you have the credits you owe me, then."

"Ah, yeah, about that." Sheni slowly sidled past them into the hanger. "Didn't you say we had until the end of the quarter? I'm pretty sure you told us we had until the quarter..."

"Yes, the *last* quarter!" Slugbarrow kept blocking Sheni's path. "I swear, if it weren't for what you did for Kapamentis, you'd all be frozen corpses circling the rings of Fomalhaut B already!"

"How very charitable of you," Gecki hissed with a sneer.

Sheni glanced across the hanger. The *Silver Hart* was docked a few bays over. Once as shiny and chrome as its name implied, their ship's hull now sported a dull, grey coat blemished with scorch marks and spots of rust. The interior was in no better condition. That was the issue with stealing a luxury starship. You couldn't afford the upkeep.

A single amphibious engineer was busy welding a panel shut on a single-seater speeder in the far corner. Otherwise, their conversation was worryingly private.

"I know you're holding out on me, lizard." Slugbarrow jabbed a pudgy finger at Gecki's smooth-scaled chest. "You've got something tasty stashed in that ship of yours, don't you? Why else won't your pilot let me on board?"

"Because they're a Xocha, man." Sheni sighed, vaguely gesturing towards the *Silver Hart's* cockpit. "You know, from Estroidea? They're extremely immunocompromised when it comes to cross-species pathogens. Rarely leaves the ship. Refuses to let *us* on sometimes."

Gecki growled deep in her throat. Slugbarrow wisely removed the offending digit from her scales and squared up to Sheni instead.

"Well, that still doesn't prove you aren't hiding something. Pay up. With interest!"

"If we had anything valuable, don't you think we'd have palmed it off on Peggi Slim already? We're telling the truth, Slugbarrow. We're broke as horses. We need more time."

"More time? *More time?*" Sheni winced as Slugbarrow's spittle peppered his face. "Other than credits you can't pay back, what else do you think I've been giving you?"

Alan pottered past all the armed goons and scampered up the *Silver Hart's* boarding ramp. Xotl unlocked the airlock doors with a hiss. They slammed shut again as soon as the little green alien was safely inside.

"Argh!" Slugbarrow screamed in frustration. "Three thousand credits! Now! Or I take your ship as compensation!"

"Stars above," Gecki rasped in horror. "It's worth twenty times that!"

"Welcome to the bailiff business, dear."

"Give us a week." Sheni smiled desperately while trying to keep a snarling Gecki from ripping the loan shark's head off. "We'll get your credits back, man, I swear."

Slugbarrow went to yell some more, then fell silent. His bulbous snout wrinkled in concentration as he figured out a way he could further profit from their misery.

"I'll give you three days," he grumbled. "But this ain't charity. That's three and a *half* thousand credits you owe me now!"

"Five days."

"*Three days*," Slugbarrow insisted. His pudgy pointing finger made a return. "Three and a half thousand credits. *And* I'm installing a tracker on your ship."

"You can't do that!" said Gecki, baring her teeth.

"Yes I freaking can, so quit your whining. It'll come off

either when you pay up, or when the *Silver Hart* belongs to me."

He clicked his fingers and one of his goons marched over to the ship. She wore a burly red backpack covered in straps. From inside one of its various pockets she pulled a black hockey puck before inputting a locking sequence on its miniature keypad. Four spider-leg clamps on its base punched through a tail wing on the *Silver Hart's* undercarriage.

Sheni winced. That wouldn't buff out.

A nod from the backpacked goon as a small red light began to blink on the tracker. Slugbarrow smirked, clapped his hands together, and waddled off in the direction of the Corpse & Casket bar with his crew.

"Three days," he shouted over his beefy shoulder. "The money or your ship. Your choice."

Gecki snarled irritably at Sheni, and then together they traipsed up to the *Silver Hart's* airlock door. The airlock doubled as a decontamination chamber. They were blasted with frigid jets before the interior set of doors slid open. Xotl waited for them on the other side.

"How did it go?" the five foot tall purple starfish asked. "Did you get Slugbarrow off our case?"

"Three and a half thousand credits in three days," Gecki growled, barging past Xotl towards the cargo hold. "May as well hand him the keys to the ship right now."

The three arms the Xocha wasn't using as legs wilted.

"I'll take that as a no, then..."

"Don't be such a downer, Gecki." Sheni jogged down the corridor after her. "We'll find a way out of this."

"You keep saying that," she snarled as she reached the hold, "like you think some guardian angel is gonna flutter down and save us. Look at this," she said, waving a clawed hand at the empty shelves. "Spare parts for the drive core. Data drives full of obsolete blueprints. Barely enough to scrape a couple hundred credits together, if that."

"So we just need to pull a real big score."

Gecki snorted.

"Good luck finding something in the next three standard rotations."

"Already got one, don't we?"

He raised an impish eyebrow. Gecki's one good eye bored into him. Then she threw her head back in exasperation.

"Two-Toes's job? Not that freakin' egg again. It's almost certainly a crock of muloch dung."

"You got any better heists lined up? Tick tock, remember?"

She scratched her chin where the scales were flaking. That happened when she got stressed.

"It's bad form to cheat a fellow pirate out of a take," she replied, albeit without much conviction.

"Come on, Gecki." Sheni grinned as he reached up and wrapped his arm around the lizard's shoulders. "We're thieves. Of *course* we can steal someone else's idea."

CHAPTER
FOUR

Through subspace the *Silver Hart* shot, a streak of grey-silver in an ocean of infinitely deep blue. Only one star occupied the sub-dimension's sky while they travelled faster than light – a lone white pinprick directly ahead of them, forever out of reach.

Sheni slipped out of his hammock in the cargo hold. The *Silver Hart* only had the one proper bedroom, but, given their recent dry spell, he probably had the most spacious sleeping quarters of everyone on board. When tired, Xotl either permitted themself to pass out in their pilot seat or cartwheeled their way down to the nest they'd cobbled together in one of the corridor's storage cubbies. Alan simply lay down and napped wherever he happened to be, which was usually the engine room. Gecki took the ship's actual bedroom, which wasn't totally unreasonable given she was the captain, not to mention the one who stole the ship. It was still kitted out with pink satin bedsheets and purple curtains. Gecki claimed she didn't have time to redecorate, but Sheni knew she secretly liked it.

He rubbed the sleep dust from his eyes with his knuckles, stretched his arms high above his head until his shoulders popped, and then headed for the stairwell leading upstairs. He paused at the bottom step. Better check on Alan first.

The engine room was, as one might expect on a starship, right at the rear of the vessel. Hot air rushed past Sheni as the door slid open. Inside the cramped forest of brass and iron, pipes clunked and the skip drive trembled in its cage. Sheni shivered despite the heat. It was a small miracle any part of the ship still worked.

That small miracle being Alan, of course.

Sheni found the green meanie tucked between two cylinders. He was tightening a valve with his favourite wrench. It had a bright red handle.

"How's it going down here?" Sheni asked, almost burning his hand on a heat shield as he squatted on his haunches. "Excited to visit Nasako?"

"Omelette," Alan gurgled obliviously.

"Yeah, you and me both. But we've got to do *something* to get us out of this hole, don't we? Can't sit around in the Corpse & Casket's docks forever."

Alan dribbled, swivelled one of his bulging eyes counter-clockwise, and got back to work. Sheni nodded resignedly.

"I guess I'll leave you to it, then."

Maybe Alan had it right, he wondered, back in the relative cool of the corridor. Blissful ignorance. It sure beat worrying about a loan shark breaking your legs. Or an irritable pirate captain pushing you out of an airlock.

Was it time to give up the free spacer life? He was starting to think he wasn't cut out for it. But what was the alternative? Earth was nothing but a charred husk. When the Arks evacuated humanity's homeworld, he hadn't been rich enough to buy a ticket or lucky enough to win one in the lottery. The only option had been to sneak on board as a stowaway. He'd been caught, obviously. Even if he hadn't, he would have run out of supplies and had to give himself up. Those in command of the Ark had elected to exile him on some barren, distant rock rather than give him a bunk. They'd had too many mouths to feed already without adding a criminal to the lunch line.

But humanity had settled on New Terra since then. A fresh homeworld full of habitable farmland. Surely they wouldn't turn him away now, not after a few years of peace and comfort away from the anxious fragility of the Arks.

Right?

But then he thought about decades spent typing at a holo-terminal from nine to five each day, inputting data for the UEC government or a corporation like Flynn Industries, and suddenly the airlock didn't sound so scary after all...

The cockpit was mercifully quieter than the engine room. It was a relatively small cockpit – certainly smaller than the cargo hold, at least – befitting a luxury ship that was only expected to house a few passengers for relatively short periods of time. The pilot's seat occupied the pointed nose at the front of the ship and was surrounded by a semi-circular dashboard full of flight sticks, buttons, dials, levers and switches, none of which Sheni understood how to use. He'd tried to learn once, and Xotl had been willing to teach him, but he couldn't even fit in the seat. It was specially designed for a Xocha's starfish-shaped physique. Xotl slotted themself into the cup with their beak at a ninety degree angle, leaving all five of their arms free to operate the controls. Xotl was a pretty decent pilot, a feat all the more impressive for that fact that their species was barely considered spacefaring at all.

Most ships ran on autopilot while a skip drive was operational, and the *Silver Hart* was no exception. The sub-dimension was pretty light on tourist spots. Xotl swivelled their chair around to face Sheni as he walked in.

Not that Xotl had a face, of course. Their beak-sphincter clacked in greeting.

"How was your nap?" they asked in a calm, deadpan voice. "I trust it left you well rested."

"Yeah, good, thanks." Sheni dropped into one of the two regular seats behind Xotl's own. "How far out from Nasako are we?"

"Our projected arrival time is one hundred and eighty six standard minutes from now. Plus an additional twenty minutes to breach the planet's atmosphere and find a suitable landing spot. Plenty of time for another nap, should you so wish."

"Nah, man, I'm plenty rested. Just itching to get this job done and pay Slugbarrow off, you know?"

"Yes, I do know. Losing this ship to him would be... severely unfortunate."

Xotl's tendency to understate things was well known amongst the rest of the crew. Unfortunate? More like catastrophic. Putting aside the difficulty he and Gecki would have procuring another ship – or hitching a ride back to Kapamentis or their respective home planets, if it came to that – Xotl would be royally screwed. It wasn't just their vulnerability to airborne diseases. Following decades of population decline, the Xocha elders had summoned every viable member of their species back to Estroidea to reproduce. Xotl refused. Like Sheni, Xotl had been permanently exiled as a result.

"Don't worry. This time tomorrow, we'll be free as birds. Trust me."

"Your optimism is contagious," Xotl replied, possibly sarcastically, turning back around to check on their dashboard.

"And extremely ill-informed, as per usual." Gecki skulked into the cockpit with a mocking sneer. "Have you even read up on where we're headed?"

"Why would I," Sheni replied as Gecki slithered into the chair opposite him, "when I know you'll do it for me?"

"Just like I do everything else," she rasped.

A wave of ice-water washed over Sheni. Gecki's sense of humour had a mean streak, but he had a suspicion she wasn't joking this time. Clearly she was still irked they'd left the space station so swiftly.

"It's not my fault humans need more sleep than you Eureptix, is it? So, go on, then. Enlighten me. What's this rock out in the boondocks got in store for us?"

Gecki sniffed haughtily.

"Nasako ain't poor, whatever people say. It just doesn't have a bunch of skyscrapers. Doesn't want them, either. The Nasakoans take a lot of pride in their culture. That includes keeping their houses, you know... *historical*."

"But we can probably assume they don't have surface-to-air missiles to shoot down wanted ships, right?"

"The *Silver Hart* isn't a wanted ship," Xotl said without turning around.

"Not yet, but it might be after we bag that egg."

"Which might not be as easy as your friend Two-Toes made out," Gecki said with a low growl. *Friend*. As if Sheni and Two-Toe Tim were friends simply because they belonged to the same species. "This ain't just some jewel they roll out for special occasions. It's practically a religious symbol."

"They think the egg is a god?" Sheni asked, raising a confused eyebrow.

"Course not," Gecki rasped. "Nasako has no state religion anymore. It's just a cultural thing. But it's real important to the people there, and not because it's reportedly made of taaffeite crystal. *Reportedly*. I don't think they give two pellets about that. There's a creature native to Nasako called a krustallos. Big flying thing. Bigger than this ship, even. Super rare, too. Local legend says seeing one grants you three cycles' good luck. And apparently, when they die, they spawn a single egg. And the Nasakoans throw a big Sunrise Ceremony to celebrate."

"It's obviously just a story, right?" Sheni smirked. "Can't imagine anything squeezing a precious gem out of its cloaca. No offence."

"You'd be surprised. But yeah, it's probably just for show. Tradition, and all that. What's important is the egg only goes on display for a couple of weeks. After that, it either hatches or it disappears somewhere no thief in the galaxy has ever managed to find. Regardless, we're working with a real small window of opportunity."

"And the ceremony only takes place approximately once every two hundred cycles," Xotl said. "You look surprised," the starfish added. "I am not Sheni. I do my own research, too."

"So it's only put on display for a few days, basically." Sheni shrugged. "Surely that's the easiest time to grab it? A few local guards we can distract with a diversion. Knock out, if they refuse to leave their posts. Easy escape back to the ship. We'll have the egg fenced and our debt paid off before tomorrow."

Gecki barked out an incredulous laugh as she picked a

strand of half-chewed protein out from between her bottom teeth.

"This ain't like robbing a museum. Curators set up all that security so they can go to bed at night assuming no-one's gonna steal anything. Which just makes the stuff easier to steal, provided you know what you're doing. In, out, nobody's the wiser 'til the morning. Nabbing something from right under everyone's snouts is a lot harder than slipping through a couple of laser grids, believe me."

"You're saying you can't do it?"

"No," she grumbled, refusing to take the bait, "I'm just saying it's hard work, that's all. Much harder work than it's worth when we could get the credits we need just by stealing a painting or two."

"Okay. Sounds good. Let's do that, then."

"Is he pulling my tail?" Gecki sat up straight and glared at Xotl, then back at Sheni. "A few hours out from the score and *now* you're open to brainstorming better suggestions?"

"What's the problem? We can always turn around, right?"

"We don't have the godsforsaken fuel!" Gecki flexed her claws. "This is just like you, Sheni. Rushing off without thinking things through."

"Sorry for thinking on my feet." Sheni performed a dramatic sigh. "I don't recall you having any bright ideas."

"If we'd taken a beat to talk things over, maybe I would have! We could have scoped out some billionaire's apartment on Kapamentis, or... or jacked a speeder from a mudball stadium's parking lot. Instead we're locked into some flight of fancy you heard about in a freakin' *bar!*"

"And how quickly do you think those plans would have landed us in a Ministerium prison cell? Kapamentis might have a lot of opportunities for criminals, but do you know what else it has a lot of? Cameras."

"And bounty hunters," Xotl added. "Whatever you two make off with, the owner needs to be somebody without deep pockets so they can't send anyone after us. I suppose that's ironic."

"Somewhere like Nasako, exactly!" Sheni beamed encouragingly at them. "Cheer up, guys. We're not even planetside and already you're acting like we're doomed. We've pulled off far more dangerous jobs than this. Just think how much that egg must be worth!"

Gecki cradled her head in her claws and groaned.

"We could simply disappear somewhere Slugbarrow can't find us," Xotl suggested. "I'm sure we could find somebody to disable the ship's tracking device, even way out in the Morg system."

"We don't have the credits," the reptilian replied, shaking her head irritably. "No, we stick with Sheni's stupid plan. And when that inevitably falls apart, we'll just crib whatever we can find. Peggi will give us good rates if we tell her what's what. We'll pay Slugbarrow however much we can scrounge together. That'll buy us some more time…"

"Unlikely," Xotl spluttered. "Faced with the choice of half the credits we owe or the *Silver Hart*, I know which one *I'd* choose."

Gecki roared and leapt up from her chair. Sheni flinched backwards. Xotl hurriedly spun their seat around to face the dashboard again.

"Gods help me! This is all your fault, Sheni. The gambling, the harebrained schemes – *all* of it. Nothing like this happened before you joined the crew."

Her yellow eye was tinged with red. She pointed a two-inch claw at Sheni's throat.

"This score of yours had better work, human. Because if we come up short, you won't need Slugbarrow to kick you off this ship. I'll throw you out myself."

CHAPTER FIVE

Gecki hadn't spoken to him like that in a long time. Despite her snarling, scaly exterior, Sheni knew Gecki to be a big softie at heart. But that threat had been genuine. If he didn't fix this, he was on his own.

She was right, of course. It *was* all his fault. He'd been the one stupid enough to lose his money on the holo-races. And then, when he'd been *assured* that the next race was a dead cert, that the drivers had all taken bribes, he'd lost the rest of the crew's takings, too. He wasn't an addict, or anything. He didn't even like the sport. It had just seemed like a smart investment at the time, what with all the guarantees the other spacers were giving him.

Instead, it left them without so much as a credit in their coffers. Unable to afford food or fuel, and still owing money to the bookmakers, they'd been forced to borrow from Slugbarrow. *Not to worry,* Sheni had told Gecki and Xotl. *The next take will be enough to pay back what we owe and leave us with change to spare.* But there hadn't been a next take. And now, thanks to him, they were about to lose it all.

Sheni sat on an empty crate in the cargo hold and scrolled the extranet on his data pad. After the argument, he didn't want to land on Nasako and still look like he hadn't a clue what he was doing. They could fix this. *He* could fix this. Put things right, whatever it took.

The *Silver Hart* lurched. A loose bolt rolled off one of the empty shelves. Sheni looked up from his data pad. They must have left subspace, which meant they'd arrived at their destination. Either that, or some other object of suitable gravitational mass had yanked them out early.

He climbed the stairs to the cockpit. Xotl had three arms on the trio of flight sticks and was using the remaining two to manage their velocity and flick switches on and off above their seat. Gecki had beaten Sheni there, having stormed off to her quarters following her earlier outburst, and was standing beside her chair. He strolled past her and took up position beside Xotl. She looked marginally less ready to bite his head off than before, but he wasn't taking any chances.

Stars glittered outside the cockpit windows. A small grey moon, scarcely any bigger than an asteroid, drifted into view. Then its planet, a rock perhaps only half the size of Earth, loomed upwards as Xotl tilted the nose of the ship down. Nasako. Half of its surface was a yellowy-brown colour with pockets of dark green; the other half was a beautiful, tranquil blue. Thick brushstrokes of white cloud swept from east to west, from daylight into the dark.

"We made good time," Sheni said, hoping an injection of positive attitude would help lighten the mood. "Fifteen minutes earlier than expected. Nice one, Xotl."

"There is always a margin of error when it comes to calculating the efficacy of skip-jumps," the starfish replied. "We were fortunate our plotted route avoided the nebula."

"Which nebula?"

"That one," Xotl said, pointing out of the window.

An enormous interstellar bruise tarnished the starboard side view. Flashes of red and electric-blue energy went off inside its dark, gaseous folds. It gave Sheni the impression of a thundercloud into which some insane general had fired hundreds of thermonuclear warheads.

"*Mon Dieu,*" he whispered, traces of his old French accent slipping through. "That thing's swallowed half the star system. Why doesn't everyone evacuate?"

"No rush," Gecki replied, a tight grip on the back of her plush chair. "It'll be eight hundred years before it starts interfering with Nasako's atmosphere. The planet will begin to crack apart another fifty years after that. It's not technically a nebula, just looks like one. Too small. Violent, though. More of a vortex. The Nasakoans call it the Purple Sunset. An ever-growing reminder of the end times."

"Otherwise known as the Sydney-Wilson Vortex," Sheni said, reading aloud from his data pad. "Huh. It's already destroyed two of the system's five planets. Can't be doing their property market much good."

"There's no stopping it," Gecki continued. "Not even the Mansa Empire can trap *that* storm in a bottle. If the system had a larger, main-sequence star, the vortex might burn itself up trying to consume it. But unfortunately, they've only got a white dwarf. The whole system will be devoured in a couple of millennia."

"And after that?"

Gecki shrugged.

"Probably just fizzle out."

"We've got clearance from Keet," Xotl gurgled, pushing two of the flight sticks forward. "Taking us down."

"I can't imagine living with something so bleak hanging over my head," Sheni mused as their ship descended.

"What, like a big cloud of debt?" Gecki gave a resentful snort. "At least *they'll* be long dead before anything bad happens."

The *Silver Hart* rocked, buffeted by the friction of Nasako's upper atmosphere. Flames began to flicker harmlessly over the cockpit windows. Sheni winced. When was the last time anyone checked the heat shields on the outside of the hull?

He turned to Gecki and, pursing his lips and avoiding eye contact, hesitantly asked a question to which he should have already known the answer.

"Humans *can* breathe Nasakoan air, right?"

Gecki's face was as hard as stone. Her thin-slitted eyes blinked slowly.

"Unfortunately, yes."

The ship continued to shake as the atmosphere outside grew denser, but the flames receded. Now all that could be seen through the windows were the outlines of continents and the wispy bands of clouds. The *Silver Hart* punched through the latter, the windows rendered a cotton wool white for a few seconds, and then below them sprawled a dusty region of craggy mountains and dry plains. To the north was a lake surrounded by a sparse tree line, and to the east, an ocean that extended beyond the horizon.

"Is that Keet?" Sheni asked Xotl, pointing down to a large settlement by the coast.

"It is indeed, Sheni. That is where the Sunrise Celebrations are being held."

"Do they get many visitors?"

"Not usually." Xotl clacked their beak together. "But

previous festivals have welcomed many curious outsiders. Our arrival likely won't be considered suspicious."

"Hopefully our departure won't either," Gecki muttered under her breath.

The settlement became a city, and the city became a grand maze of domed houses, zigzagging streets and cracked towers of bleached stone, all drenched in golden midday sun. It wasn't opulent, by any means – and it certainly lacked the technology present in the Corpse & Casket, let alone a city-planet like Kapamentis – but it was rich with culture and storied history. They passed a bunch of yellow and purple balloons drifting up over the tallest buildings as the *Silver Hart* came in to land.

"Do we need a docking permit or anything?" Sheni asked. It was bad enough that the *Silver Hart* had been logged as entering Nasakoan airspace. The less evidence they left behind, the better.

"I shouldn't think so." Xotl flapped their 'topmost' arm around to peer at him. Xocha had eyes in each of their five limbs, apparently, and as many again around their beaks, though all Sheni could make out was a dense pattern of suckers. "This isn't one of the inner systems. Docking should be free. But if not, I can always set the ship down outside the city limits."

True enough, three ports in Keet offered free docking. One was already full with trader ships, so out of the remaining two Xotl set the *Silver Hart* down in the one closest to the hub of the celebrations. The ship sagged onto her landing gear and her engines switched off with a staggered groan.

"Okay." Sheni clapped his hands together and grinned. "Game plan. Let's find out where they've got this egg on show, scope the joint out, and then figure out a way to grab it. I'm thinking you and me, Gecki, we can—"

Something brushed his leg. Alan stood between him and Gecki, his wonky eyes fixed on two separate points to either side of Sheni's shoulders. The ends of his vacant smile threatened to extend beyond the limits of his little green face. He was still holding his favourite wrench, the one with the red handle.

"Erm... well, hey! I guess Alan is coming, too."

One of Alan's eyes rolled slowly upwards to stare at the ceiling. A tiny bubble of drool popped in the corner of his mouth.

"He's a liability," Gecki growled.

"Don't be like that, you big grump." Sheni patted Alan on the head. "There's no harm in him tagging along while we're just scouting the place, is there?"

Gecki rasped something incomprehensible to herself as she stomped off in the direction of the airlock. Sheni turned back to Xotl and winked.

"Don't let the drive cores get too cool," he said, ushering Alan through the door. "Gecki can be as cynical as she likes, but I'm telling you – this job's gonna be a *cinch*."

CHAPTER SIX

The heat hit Sheni the moment he stepped out of the airlock. Thirty-two degrees Celsius, according to his data pad. He was sweating already. The cold, recycled air on board the *Silver Hart* and the Corpse & Casket had made him soft.

"Oof," he said, fanning himself with his hand. "That's a bit much, you know?"

"Speak for yourself," Gecki said, squinting her eyes as she basked her chest in the sun. "I think it feels just fine."

The port was barebones – just a dusty patch of nothing with four landing platforms set into the cracked earth. The small buildings around the perimeter swam in a rippling haze. One other ship was docked alongside them – a small, personal cruiser with just enough space for two passengers and their luggage. It was certainly worth more than the three and a half thousand credits they owed Slugbarrow, but getting into it would attract a lot of unnecessary attention. Plus, every set of thrusters was centrally registered and easily traceable. No way would Peggi Slim accept it, not in its present state. Despite Gecki's suggestions when trying to come up with alternative means of paying off their debt, grand theft auto really wasn't their crew's style. Neither was stranding some poor stranger on an alien world.

Sheni shielded his eyes with his hand. Nasako's star may have been small and in the final stage of its lifecycle, but Nasako was only the second planet out. At least this was as hot as the day would get. Still, he was going to get one hell of a headache if he didn't find shade soon.

After making sure Alan hadn't got himself stuck between the metal steps leading down from the landing platform, they set off towards the sounds of revelry and joy.

Two older Nasakoans sat on rickety wooden chairs under a straw umbrella by the exit. Their bald, desert sand-coloured heads were covered in liver spots and their tendril beards looked like shrivelled up worms. They broke into friendly, toothless smiles as Sheni passed. He reckoned they were there to keep an eye on people's ships, but he wasn't particularly worried about parking the *Silver Hart* anywhere. Xotl hadn't left the ship unattended in years. They used to have some pretty decent armaments installed, too – unregistered, of course – but those had all been sold off long before they found themselves in financial trouble.

The first set of buildings they passed – single storey clay huts with wooden doors and round shutters over the windows – weren't tall enough for their shadows to offer much in the way of shade. Sheni pulled the flask from his pocket, raised it to his lips, then paused. He gave it a sniff and relaxed. Yes, it was water. He had a habit of filling the flask with booze and then forgetting about it. Right now, however, their alcohol reserves were about as empty as their purse.

"Want some?" he said, offering the flask to Gecki.

"Nah, I'm good," the lizard rasped. "I want my scales to dry out. Helps with the shedding."

Sheni shivered as he imagined waking up in the dead of night to find a translucent, Gecki-shaped skin-suit left in a corner of the ship.

The further they walked, the more lively Keet became. Small eggs, painted in bright colours and patterns by the local children, started appearing in the windows of people's homes. Nasakoans sat on doorsteps and staircases, sharing jokes and platters of home cooked delicacies. Yellow banners and streamers hung suspended between neighbouring houses. From the relieved smiles on people's faces, Sheni would have assumed their nation was celebrating the end of a particularly arduous war, not waiting for an egg to hatch.

Dozens of paths, each as narrow and wonky as the last, split off to form a residential labyrinth. But there was no question of which direction to head in. They only had to follow the music. The ground rumbled with its beat. Someone was having one hell of a party.

"So, I've been thinking," Sheni whispered to Gecki as they pushed through a curtain of rainbow ribbons. "This crystal egg, right, it's revered. So I figure it's got to be kept somewhere *fairly* quiet, you know? Why don't we—"

They stopped short. Sheni had seen plenty of protests on Earth before the mass exodus, but he only remembered a few being as densely populated as this. Thankfully, this crowd was throwing flowers and shapes, not bottles and bricks. A range of percussive instruments were being pounded, generally in time with one another though sometimes delayed by the distance between bands. Soothing steel bowls, snappier snares, the deep boom of war drums. Whistling woodwinds and scorching synths battled one another for melodic prominence. Colourful clouds of powder exploded upwards, accompanied by excited whoops and cheers from the dancing festival goers. Most were Nasakoans, but Sheni spotted feathered Argentans, slender blue Oortilians, and a pair of gelatinous Kwoo Fim amongst the crowd, too.

The clay dwellings became taller, grew wooden extensions, swelled together in rolling hills. Shops gave out free samples; houses were opened to strangers and friends alike; stalls had been hastily cobbled together by generous local patrons. And far on the other side of the energetic celebrations stood a grand temple built into a sheer cliff face of sandstone. The sharp glint of something bejewelled within its columns caught Sheni's eye.

Gecki turned to him with a sly smirk on her face.

"What were you just saying? Maybe it's best you leave the thinking to me, yeah?"

Sheni grumbled and bent down with his hands on his thighs to speak to Alan.

"What do you say, little guy? Fancy taking a—"

Alan sprinted off into the crowds, arms raised above his head like half-cooked spaghetti, gurgling and muttering to himself with excitement.

"And... he's gone."

"I told you not to bring him. He's a hindrance."

"Oh, stop it. That hindrance is as much a part of the crew as the rest of us. We'd both be dead twice over if it weren't for Alan."

Gecki huffed through her flared nostrils.

"Let's just find this stupid egg of yours."

They could barely push through the throng. Nasakoans weren't big people, but they sure didn't leave a lot of room for personal space. Sheni felt more than one set of tendrils brush his exposed forearms. It seemed like every citizen in the city – and probably from a great deal of other settlements on Nasako, too – had turned up for the party.

He was engulfed by a cloud of steam that smelled of pork, salt and hot spices. Somebody was barbecuing meat on a big silver grill. Sheni's stomach rumbled even though he knew it wasn't *really* pig meat, and he wished he had enough credits to buy something. Then he watched the locals interact with the stall. The vendor was wrapping the pork up in edible leaves and handing out packets for free. Sheni approached the grill and, much to his surprise, was treated as if he were a Nasakoan, too. Even Gecki graciously accepted a packet. Sheni wolfed his down in three bites and licked his fingers clean. Freakin' delicious.

Sheni was glad to have finished his food so quickly, because only a few stalls down was an enormous rack that stank terribly of fish. He didn't know how everyone else could stand it; the pungent odour made him retch. The Nasakoans didn't have protruding noses like a human, but they definitely possessed nostrils. Stars above. The collection of sea creatures – caught in the neighbouring ocean, Sheni was sure – was more diverse than the passengers of a Kapamentis transit shuttle. Twelve foot eels as black as the cosmos; angler fish with teeth like acupuncture needles; a huge salmon-like thing covered in sickly green boils. He quickly made a beeline in the opposite direction. Despite her normally robust constitution, Gecki was just as keen to follow.

They passed bars handing out paper cups of ale and fruit punch. Sheni was tempted to try some, but just about kept himself in check. As fun as the festival was, they were in Keet for a job. He didn't know how watered-down the free drinks were, but he needed to keep a clear head – even if only to keep Gecki off his back.

A Nasakoan played a drum-like instrument formed of fifteen electronic pads. Each time she hit one with her hands, it let out a haunting wail like a spectre calling out from a marsh. Sheni quite liked the tones it made, but he couldn't see how they fit the mood of the festival. Then again, he was human. Not every species interpreted colours and sounds the same way he did. A dozen metres further on, a group of local children gathered around a crude copper pipe jutting out of the ground. They ducked and covered their ear-holes with their hands as a rocket screeched out of the pipe and exploded above them in a cloud of dry, purple paint. Sheni jumped but everybody else laughed, especially the children. Not every species shared the same basic child safety laws, either.

An elderly trader waved him over to a stand drenched in flamboyant bouquets. Sheni pointed to himself as he pushed his way through the crowd. She nodded joyfully and then draped a beautiful garland of yellow and purple flowers around his neck.

"Why all the yellow and purple, if you don't mind me asking?" He rubbed the silky petals between his thumb and forefinger. "I keep seeing these two colours everywhere."

"Yellow for the sunrise," the old Nasakoan woman replied enthusiastically. She pointed a frail finger to the sky. "Purple for the sunset."

Sheni followed the finger while the attendant fetched another garland. The nebulous vortex occupied almost a quarter of Nasako's sky. He hadn't noticed how visible it was before, what with the midday sun being so unbearably bright.

The stall owner tried to loop the garland around Gecki's

neck, but she wasn't tall enough to reach. Gecki took a step backward, teeth bared.

"No, thanks. I'm not keen on collars."

"Go on," Sheni insisted, biting his lip in glee. "It's customary. We want to fit in, don't we?"

Gecki fixed him with a fiery glare and then dutifully lowered her head. The only item of clothing she ever wore was her tired, brown leather jacket, and even then it was mostly just for the pockets. Attire got in the way of her camouflage ability, and her reptilian species had no hang-ups regarding nudity. The ring of flowers added the first splash of colour he'd seen on her in years.

"I think it suits you," Sheni said as they left the stall.

"One flick of my claw and your entrails are steaming on the floor," she snarled.

"I assumed they'd be nervous about the Big Bad Bruise in the sky," he said, quickly changing topic. "But they seem to celebrate it almost as much as they do this mythical krustallos of theirs. Doesn't that strike you as odd?"

"Course it does," she replied. "But that's coz we're new to it. *They've* all been living with the vortex since they were hatched. Or birthed, or however it is their species comes into this galaxy. The eventual destruction of their planet is just a fact of life, same as it was for every one of their ancestors since Nasakoan civilisation began."

"I suppose it's not hurting anyone today, is it?" Sheni nudged Gecki in the ribs with his elbow. "Stop worrying about tomorrow, right? Maybe you could learn a thing or two from them."

"Accepting that your planet has an expiry date eight hundred years from now is not the same as blindly stumbling through life believing your mistakes don't have consequences." Gecki grabbed Sheni's shoulder and spun him around to face her. "The Nasakoans are pragmatic. You, human, are just stupid."

She craned her neck to look above the heads of the partying locals.

"The temple is just over there," she snapped. "I suggest we get in line."

The crowd grew denser and denser still, until they reached a point where it was impossible to push any further through without drawing irritated glances from all the other tourists and pilgrims. They waited their turn as the herd gradually funnelled towards the base of a very wide set of wooden steps. Barriers of frayed rope regulated the visitors' ascent. Gecki had her arms crossed and kept tapping her claws against her scales. Clearly Slugbarrow's deadline played heavily on her mind.

"Look, I'm sorry, all right?" Sheni whispered. "I messed up. But it's not like we owe Slugbarrow half a million credits. We'll get through this. Promise."

Gecki let out a heavy sigh.

"I don't care that you lost credits on the holo-races. You got tricked. Crud happens. What riles me up is you lost *my* credits, and Xotl's, and Alan's, not that I'm sure he knows what currency is. You put everyone's livelihood at risk. Our *lives*, maybe, if we lose the ship. You know Xotl can't survive in a regular atmosphere. And it's all because you never think. You rush ahead without a plan. You assume you'll always come up smelling of roses. But the galaxy stinks, Sheni. It's dangerous. There's a cost to living recklessly, but it's the rest of us who pay the price."

They shuffled up the steps.

"I get it, you know?" Sheni's shoulders sagged. "And hey, I won't take a cut of this score. Or the next one, or however many it takes until I pay back what I lost. Just don't drop me from the crew, Gecki. You need me."

"Like a scale needs rot," she scoffed. "And a cut? When have any of us ever taken a *cut*? We're always living claw to mouth as it is. I dunno, Sheni. Times are hard. We never had these problems... before..."

Gecki's words trailed off as she climbed another step and the Cradle of the Krustallos finally came into view. Diamonds sparkled in the black slit of her wide yellow eye.

"Yeah." Sheni broke into a mischievous grin. "Not so pissed off now, huh?"

"That," Gecki replied numbly, "is one godsdamn shiny egg."

CHAPTER SEVEN

Even in the shade cast by the columns, the egg positively shone. The closer they got to the top of the steps, the more glimpses of it they got through the gradually diminishing queue.

"So." Sheni rubbed his hands together. "How much do you think that much taaffeite crystal goes for?"

"Fifty, maybe sixty thousand?" Gecki inhaled sharply. She still had that sparkly, faraway look in her eyes. "Could be six figures, though. You don't normally see intact gems that big."

A paint-rocket detonated in the air behind them, pulling her out of her daydream.

"Two-Toes is gonna be so pissed," she rasped cautiously. "Daft sod's fault for running his mouth about it in a damn pirate bar."

"We could always be nice and give him a cut of the take. Say, ten percent. Call it a finder's fee, you know?"

They looked blankly at one another, then burst into laughter.

"Think what we could do with that many credits," Sheni

continued. "Pay off Slugbarrow, obviously. Buy a round or two at the Corpse & Casket. But we could properly invest in the *Silver Hart*, too. Get her looking her old self again."

"Imagine the bender we could carve through Kapamentis," Gecki mused, before adding, "Better keep you away from the casino moons, though..."

"We could even go legit if we wanted. Start a trader business or something, you know? Get out of the pirate game for good."

"Pah! Let's not get ahead of ourselves. We still have to steal the freakin' thing."

Sheni felt an odd presence beside his leg. He looked down and snorted with amusement.

"Look who found his way back to us. Somebody's sure had fun."

Alan smiled beside them like a happy green pug dog. He was wearing a flowery garland like theirs, but it was too big for him and hung off one shoulder like a Miss World's sash. Somebody had painted his face with purple stripes. A stringy bracelet of petals and pebbles dangled from the raised head of his wrench.

"Excuse me," a timid Nasakoan behind them said, tapping Sheni on the shoulder, "but I think he just jumped the line..."

"He's been standing with us the whole time," Gecki snarled, spinning around with drool stringing between her razor-sharp teeth.

"Oh, so he has," the Nasakoan quickly replied, dropping their eyes to the floor. "My mistake."

They reached the top of the steps. Their group was next in the queue. Those ahead obscured Sheni's view of the egg itself, but he got a good look at the surrounding stage. Wide, empty, wooden, flanked by ornately carved sandstone columns and the occasional flaming torch on a pole. The three narrow cave mouths in the cliff face at the back presumably led to subterranean caverns – the temple proper. Two guards with electrically-charged pikes protected the egg, another stood watch beside each entrance to the temple, and one more kept the line in check.

Easy enough for a modest mercenary group to overpower. Not so simple for three misfits just looking for a way to keep a loan shark from breaking their fingers.

"Next," the guard beside the queue announced, pulling aside the final stretch of rope barrier. Sheni, Gecki and Alan shuffled forwards as the previous group departed back down the creaking steps.

"Be honest, Gecki," Sheni whispered. "Tell me this wasn't worth the flight here."

A cushioned plinth of millennia-old metal stood alone on the stage. Four clamps rose from around the purple cushion, and clutched in their grasp was the most resplendent gemstone Sheni had ever seen. Two-Toe Tim hadn't quite got the size right – it was larger than an ostrich egg, probably coming all the way up to Sheni's knees. Light coruscated across its sharp, crystalline edges like it were the stone of a million carat engagement ring. No matter how far past the security barrier he leaned, or how hard he squinted, he couldn't quite see through to its centre.

"Oh, it's something, all right." Gecki stalked around the egg, inspecting it from every angle. "The way it refracts the light... I've never seen taaffeite so clear."

"I guess that makes it even more valuable, right?" Sheni sidled up beside her and whispered, "Do you think we can just lift it off?"

"I couldn't. You *definitely* can't. You see those clamps? Pressure-locked tungsten. Nobody's getting that egg off without a diamond-tipped laser cutter. Or, you know, the key."

"Key? I don't see a keyhole."

"The circular indentation at the front. Something slots in there. Looks simple, but check out all those tiny grooves. Only the original device will work."

"And we can't just smash the egg and gather up the pieces?"

"What, and cut the market value in half? Nah, you'd have better luck breaking the clamps. Besides, I reckon people might notice us taking a sledgehammer to their magic crystal."

Sheni considered the queue stretching out behind them. He couldn't imagine this part of town grew totally quiet even in the dead of night.

"So it's the key or nothing, then." A thought struck Sheni. He spun around on the spot. "Erm, have you seen Alan?"

Gecki growled in the negative. Sheni turned back to the plinth and almost suffered a heart attack.

"Stars above... Alan, get down from there!"

Alan was balanced precariously atop the egg. He tapped it gently with the head of his wrench. The crystal gave off a high pitched *ting* like a fork hitting a wine glass.

"Hydrocrystalophone," he gurgled gleefully.

The furious guards snapped to attention and charged towards the Cradle. Their pikes ignited with forks of blue lightning.

"Good gods," Sheni stepped over the barrier and yanked Alan back down. "I am so sorry," he said to everyone around them. "We were just leaving."

They hurried back down the steps and into the shocked crowd before any of the guards could grab them. Nasakoans queuing the other way gasped and whispered to one another in hushed, appalled voices. Sheni gritted his teeth. So much for keeping a low profile.

When he stopped and looked at Gecki, she was fixing him with a telling stare.

"Yes, liability, fine." He grabbed Alan's hand to keep him from running off again. "At least we found out the guards aren't all that."

"Well, we can count on them being on high alert now, can't we?" Gecki scratched at the flaky scales under her chin. "Ah, we've faced worse. Just need to find that key."

Sheni smiled to himself. He could always trust something shiny to turn Gecki's mood around.

"Who do you think has it? One of the guards up on the stage?"

"Bit risky. I'd keep it secure in a safe somewhere, then give the key to *that* lock to someone senior who ain't near the egg all day. But that's just me."

A roar of excitement rippled through the festival. At first Sheni assumed another paint rocket had been set off, or perhaps a new musician was about to perform, but then he noticed a procession of banners – primarily yellow and purple, of course – jostling about above everyone's heads.

He jabbed a thumb in the direction of the hullabaloo and raised a suggestive pair of eyebrows.

"Worth checking out?"

Gecki nodded, running her forked tongue over her teeth in deep thought.

They pushed through the crowd once more. Many people were cheering. A few were clapping, too. Was the egg being moved to a safer location following Alan's little 'indiscretion'? Sheni wondered whether stashing the gem in a vault away from the prying eyes of the public would make it easier for their crew to steal, or harder.

As with the queue leading to the temple, there came a point where squeezing through attendees was no longer an option. Sheni could make out the banners a lot better now, plus the streamers and ribbons making their poles look like lemon and blackcurrant candy canes, but he still didn't have a great view of the procession itself. It sounded important. He didn't want to miss it.

Gecki tapped a claw on his shoulder, then pointed up to their left. A bridge, erected for the festival in a hurry using what looked like driftwood from the nearby shore, linked the second storeys of a pair of clay houses. A few local Nasakoan children, their beard-tendrils barely more than fleshy nubs, sat with their bare feet dangling over the edge.

They retreated to the bridge. Gecki climbed onto a neighbouring skip and then heaved herself up onto the tottering structure. It creaked and groaned beneath her weight, but Sheni knew better than to pass comment. He lifted Alan up to Gecki – they couldn't risk him performing another disappearing act, or attempting to crack open the egg a second time – and then clambered up beside them. The boards swayed precariously beneath their feet – not that any of the children sitting on the bridge appeared to notice.

"Much better," Sheni said, arms out wide, struggling to keep his balance.

He could see all eight Nasakoans in the procession now. Most of them looked like medieval monks, their brown robes speckled with dust, weighty hoods shielding their faces from the harsh sun. Six of the monks carried a banner each and, judging by the few dour expressions Sheni could make out, took their roles very seriously indeed. Another held a small drum under one arm and was beating it with a rag-wrapped mallet.

The eighth member of the parade wore a paler robe with its hood pulled back. He looked much older and much friendlier than his companions, holding a golden sceptre in one hand like a walking stick while waving convivially at the crowds with the other.

"Who's that guy?" Sheni asked no-one in particular.

"That's High Priest Szaladar," one of the children sitting on the edge of the bridge said, looking over her shoulder with an expression of pure repulsion. "*Duh*."

"Oh, yeah?" Sheni crouched down beside her and smiled as toothily as possible. "And what does *he* do?"

"He's in charge of the Sunrise Temple and he has a seat on the city council and he kicks off all the festivals with these big, boring speeches." The child tutted and went back to watching the procession. "Only *idiots* don't know that."

Well, that sure put him in his place.

"Check out that Szaladar guy's staff," Gecki rasped quietly as he stood back up. "Anything look familiar to you?"

"Gold, isn't it? Might just be plating, but still. Reckon we should steal it?"

"Yes, but not for that reason." Gecki rolled her eyes. "Look what's at the top."

Sheni squinted. A large, circular medallion was pinned onto a pair of gold wings. It looked valuable. Had some sort of fancy dragon creature embossed on its face and everything.

"The key," he said suddenly. "That medallion – it must be what operates the clamps on the plinth!"

"Again, *duh*," said the little girl by their feet. She

scrunched up her face. "Like, how do you not know all of this?"

"And how do *you* not know that my species likes to eat snotty brats who don't mind their own business?" Gecki growled, smiling widely.

The kid snapped her mouth shut.

"Can we climb down now?" Sheni could feel the planks of the bridge start to sag. "I think we got all we came to see."

As soon as they were back on solid ground, Gecki stuck out her hand.

"Give me your data pad."

"Erm, why?"

"Because," she said, grabbing his device and tapping at the screen with a claw, "I need to look up Keet's municipal building. A guy as busy as Szaladar's got to have an office, right?"

"Sure, I guess..." Sheni's brow furrowed. "But how does that help us get the medallion?"

She shrugged. "He has to put the staff down sometime, doesn't he?"

"To go to the bathroom, maybe. Or to bed." He tried peering over Gecki's shoulder. "I don't get it. Do you plan on making an appointment, or...?"

Gecki turned the data pad around and pointed at the address on the screen.

"I was thinking we could just drop in," she said with a roguish grin.

CHAPTER EIGHT

Sheni stood in the lobby of the Keet Council Centre trying to look inconspicuous, which was challenging enough as a man without tentacles on his face without the added task of keeping Alan from climbing the rafters.

"We're in position," he said in a voice barely above a whisper. "You inside yet?"

The council building was situated much further from the coastline, away from the shops and homes clustered around the temple. The address Gecki found on Sheni's data pad hadn't been entirely useful, because it turned out the Nasakoans didn't signpost their streets particularly often. Or sometimes even name their alleyways, for that matter. Fortunately, they had a backup plan. The excitement accompanying the High Priest's procession made tracking Szaladar down again very simple, and eventually they followed him to a three storey structure of old sandstone walls and wooden scaffolding Gecki recognised from the extranet pictures.

The lobby occupying most of the ground floor was fairly

quiet, in stark contrast to the widespread partying taking place outside. The bleeps and bloops of electronic music and the thick smell of something sugary wafted through the open doors. Sheni got a few curious looks from the Nasakoans still working in the building, but he received a similar number of friendly smiles, too. He had his cover story lined up in case anyone asked why he was hanging about by himself. His crew were interested in setting up a trade link between Kapamentis and the local market vendors, and his colleague was upstairs enquiring about permits.

"On my way up now," Gecki replied, her gravelly voice speaking through Sheni's earpiece. "Had to wait for the alley to clear."

"Remind me again what we're looking for?"

"What *I'm* looking for, you mean. Your job is to keep watch in case our holy friend heads back upstairs."

"Right, but that's just it, isn't it? We need that golden disc to unlock the egg. And unless the sunstroke is making me see things, Szaladar still has it."

They'd followed the High Priest until he disappeared into his office on the second floor of the Council Centre. When he reappeared half an hour later, clutching a battered, old digi-tablet under one arm, he still had the golden sceptre with him – and with it, the medallion. He was presently one of the few Nasakoans standing on the opposite side of the lobby to Sheni, talking politics with another pair of white-haired council members who looked nearly as ancient as he did.

"Sure," Gecki replied, "but he could have a spare locked away, couldn't he? Or a rota for the guards, or something. It's called reconnaissance, Sheni. It's what professionals do."

"And if there isn't a spare? That medallion looks pretty bespoke, Gecki."

"Gah! Even a High Priest has to sleep sometime. We wait 'til he's home, take the whole godsdamn staff if we have to, and then snatch that egg under the cover of darkness. Is that a sensible enough plan for you, or would you prefer to tackle the old man to the floor and snatch the medallion while everyone's watching?"

Sheni grumbled to himself. Of *course* they had to be careful and play the cards they were dealt. He was just worried they were taking too long, that's all. They came to Nasako to grab a big gemstone. Two-Toes had made it sound simple. Now they had *two* things to steal, and they were still no closer to paying Slugbarrow back than when they started.

This wasn't the time for reconnaissance. This was the time for action.

Plus, he was starting to feel a little bad about the whole thing. Not that he'd admit it to Gecki, of course, not after dragging her halfway across the galaxy. From what little he'd seen of the local culture, the Nasakoans were good people. They led simple lives compared to those in the inner systems, but were all the happier for it. Sheni didn't exactly feel great about stealing their sacred artefact, even if they probably didn't appreciate just how many credits the damn thing was worth.

But, you know... desperate times, and all that.

You do what you have to do, right?

Gecki snarled to herself as she slithered up the alleyside wall of the municipal building. Typical Sheni, asking stupid questions while she did all the hard work.

The sandstone irritated her stomach, but she had to keep close. The further she protruded from the building, the greater the chance someone would notice her climbing it. She could only change the colour of her scales to match her surroundings, not *actually* render herself invisible. That said, a yellow-brown exterior wall was considerably easier to mimic than a cargo hold bulging with treasure, and that had never posed her too much trouble either.

Her claws scraped the stone while the tiny hairs on her toe pads kept her from coming unstuck. A quick glance back down. Somebody was strolling along the alley below, but there was no urgency to their pace. They hadn't seen her. At this point, even if they looked up they'd probably dismiss her as just a trick of the heat haze.

The High Priest's office was on the second floor. They'd followed him up through the inside of the building but had stopped short of knocking on his office door after he'd gone inside. It wasn't hard to calculate which was the corresponding window. A pair of scuffed wooden shutters had been drawn across it to block out the afternoon sun.

On some planets, Gecki would have been faced with unbreakable (and probably blacked-out) glass, or even a miniature forcefield that could only be deactivated from inside. Not on Nasako, however. They liked to let the air in. And she couldn't blame them. So close to the shore, it was godsdamn crisp.

She curled a sharp claw around the edge of the shutters, pried them open, and crawled in.

Even Gecki, an undeniably cold-blooded reptile, found

the coolness of the office refreshing after so long spent baking outdoors. She shook herself in her species' equivalent of a shiver and gave her eyes a moment to adjust to the dimness of the room.

Huh. Szaladar was one messy priest.

Papers littered the floor. Many species had long since moved onto almost exclusively digital forms of communication and record-keeping, but a few preferred to keep things tactile. In a galaxy full of cyberpunks and console-jockeys, it wasn't always such a terrible idea. A bookcase of dusty tomes had been upended. Small clay statues had been knocked off the shelves; a few had smashed in the fall. A computer terminal, ancient by the *Silver Hart's* standards, sat on top of a sandalwood desk. It didn't appear to have a source of power. Gecki glanced behind its chunky monitor. Someone had pulled out all the wires.

There were two doors in the office, and both of them were cracked open. One led into the corridor where Gecki, Sheni and Alan had stood only half an hour before. The other was a mystery. She edged closer, her claws primed to slash and maul, and then quickly threw the door open. It was just a private toilet. Towels and spare robes had been stored in the cupboard opposite, but these too were now spilled over the floor.

Gecki returned to the main room and re-opened comms.

"Sheni, can you hear me?"

"Loud and clear, Gecki."

"Does the priest look flustered to you? Like he's in a rush to be somewhere else, or something?"

"Erm, no? He's smiling and laughing. Why?"

"Yeah, I was hoping this weren't the case. Somebody got here before us."

"What? Who?"

"Don't know, but the place is trashed. Give me a moment to figure this out..."

Sheni continued to complain in her ear, but Gecki ignored him. Somebody had broken into High Priest Szaladar's office right before she could. As far as she was concerned, that meant one of two things. Either the priest had got himself mixed up in something dodgy, or they weren't the only ones looking to steal that krustallos egg.

And the priest didn't seem the dodgy kind.

She pulled open the drawers of his desk, rummaged through the documents spread out in a blanket on the floor, rifled through the pages of his tomes in case anything was hidden inside. But no matter how hard she searched, she couldn't find anything pertaining to that damn medallion.

"—on his way!"

"What are you prattling on about?" she snarled.

"The High Priest," Sheni hissed. "He's finished talking to those councillors and he's headed back upstairs!"

"Then stop him, you cretin! I am *not* taking the fall for this mess!"

Down on the ground floor, Sheni suddenly felt far hotter than he had back in the festival. Szaladar was crossing the lobby, glancing down at the digi-tablet still cradled in one arm, the bottom of his staff tapping the hard floor with the steady tick-tock of a grandfather clock.

Time was most certainly running out.

"Excuse me, sir?" Sheni said loud enough to attract the attention of a few other Nasakoans working in the lobby. "High Priest Szaladar, can I have a word?"

The priest paused just short of the grand staircase and

gave Sheni a look of surprise. Yet despite his momentary confusion, Szaladar's smile never entirely left his lips. He took a couple of shuffling steps towards Sheni, who was striding across the lobby to meet him with Alan in tow.

"Certainly, young man," he said, nodding graciously. "I must say, I don't believe I've ever had the pleasure of meeting someone from your species before. Kerulian, is it? Did you come all this way just for the Sunrise Celebrations?"

"Human, actually. And yes, we did. This little guy's a big fan. When he heard there was a hatching soon, well... there was no way we were gonna miss it!"

With a crack of his back, High Priest Szaladar bent down to look Alan in the eye. He could only manage one. The other was staring at a tulip-shaped lamp hanging on the wall.

"And what's your name, little one?"

"Simon," Alan gurgled vacantly.

"Well, Simon, thank you *very* much for coming. I hope you stay to witness the final ceremony. It is such a rare and special event. Your, ahem, *father* must care about you a great deal to bring you all this way."

Sheni glanced at the sceptre. A bead of sweat rolled down his temple. The medallion was so close. He could even see the grooves and teeth that turned the Cradle's locking mechanism around its edge. All he had to do was reach out and unclip it without anyone noticing...

Szaladar stood up straight again, a painful process that sounded like branches of birch being snapped in half, and smiled politely at Sheni.

"Morning's blessings on you both," he said, before turning back to the staircase.

Sheni panicked. He hadn't bought Gecki anywhere near enough time.

"One more thing, Mr. High Priest," he said, chasing after him. "Some of the food and drink in that festival of yours is fantastic. Real good brand potential, you know? I wonder if I could bend your ear a while to discuss franchising..."

Gah! The High Priest's office was so godsdamn simple. No safes, no locked cupboards, no secret floorboard compartments. There wasn't enough space to hide a bracelet, let alone an eight inch medallion!

Sheni could talk the ears off an elephant, but Szaladar was a politician as well as a priest. He'd shrug him off and come upstairs eventually. She didn't have long. And Gecki wasn't going to tidy up the man's office for him. The old guy would realise somebody had ransacked the place and raise the alarm. This whole operation was turning to crud.

She was frantically rummaging through the drawers of the desk when a document beside the defunct computer terminal caught her eye. She snatched it up. It was some sort of invoice. Looked like it had been issued by a local business, an assumption given weight by the document's paper nature. Curious, very curious...

The door to the office creaked open.

It wasn't High Priest Szaladar. It wasn't anybody from his order, either – Gecki was pretty certain of that. The figure standing in the doorway was a Kerulian, a species similar in appearance to humans except for the bony ridges that ran along the top of their skulls and the tufts of feathers that sprouted from their temples. He wore spacer leathers in need of a good scrub. Silver rings hung from his pointy ears.

"Ah," Gecki snarled with a tilt of her head. "Came back for another look, is that it?"

She wasn't sure if the Kerulian thought she was a rival pirate or a member of Szaladar's non-existent security detail, but he pulled a snub-nose laser pistol on her all the same. Gecki was quick for her size. She dodged to the right just as he fired. The shot screeched past her and burned a small, round hole through the window shutters.

By the time Gecki propelled herself off the right-hand wall of the office towards him, the Kerulian had left the doorway. Her leg clipped the door, slamming it shut. It was just the two of them for the moment, though only the gods knew how many others in the office had heard that gunshot.

He tried for another. Gecki swatted the pistol out of his hands and it clattered underneath Szaladar's desk. The pirate darted for it. Gecki stuck out her other arm and slammed him backward into the opposite wall.

Despite the disparity between their species' strength, the Kerulian wasn't giving up. He punched Gecki in the gut, then the mouth. The hit to her stomach was worse, even managing to wind her slightly. The punch to her mouth probably did more damage to his fist than her face, and she could regrow lost teeth anyway.

She punched him in the jaw. Something cracked. *That* wasn't going to heal on its own. They were pinned against the wall together, practically dancing. Well, dancing the way Eureptix partners did, anyway.

The Kerulian pulled a knife. She should have expected it. He plunged it toward her ribcage. Too fast and low for her to block. Fortunately, his angle was all wrong. The blade skimmed across her scales rather than through them, summoning a thin, red line of blood.

Gecki roared. Time to wrap this up.

She grabbed his hand and twisted. Another loud crack. Then, as the pirate screamed in pain, she took his head in both hands and slammed it against the wall.

Maybe she shoved him harder than she anticipated. Maybe Nasakoan walls weren't that sturdy. Either way, the Kerulian's head ended up in a different room to the rest of him.

Gecki opened the door to the adjoining bathroom and checked on her assailant's status. Yep, definitely dead. Humanoid craniums weren't supposed to be that shape. She didn't feel any remorse. It was his fault for pulling a gun. The idiot could have run instead.

There was a marking on the back of the pirate's neck. It looked like a welt, or something – like he'd been burnt. She hooked a claw around the man's collar and peeled it back.

Not a welt, exactly. A clan brand.

An alien skull set against the backdrop of a lightning bolt.

Yeah, there was no mistaking *that* insignia. She'd seen it around the Corpse & Casket a few times. It was the sort of design any sensible spacer steered clear of.

Thunderskull.

"I guess we're not the only thieves in town," she growled to herself. "Freakin' brilliant."

Footsteps coming down the corridor outside. Even if the Nasakoans working in the building had somehow dismissed the gunshot for a firework, there was no mistaking the subsequent scuffle. She'd better make herself scarce.

Remembering to take the curious invoice she found, Gecki slithered back out through the window, closing the mildly singed shutters behind her.

CHAPTER NINE

The sun began to set on Keet. Golden light turned to amber. A band of midnight black beckoned over the horizon.

Xotl ignited the *Silver Hart's* vertical thrusters and ascended over the city. They weren't worried about losing their parking spot. There wasn't exactly a rush for spaces.

Thunderskull's ship wasn't in Keet – that much they knew already. His flagship was far too big to land within most metropolitan areas, especially ones with such close-knit infrastructure. It was quite possible that Thunderskull himself wasn't even on Nasako, that he'd just sent a small schooner to scout out the area and grab the egg for him. He was a notorious pirate captain, after all. But if Sheni and Gecki's own heist was to go ahead, they had to be sure.

It was evident even from down on the ground that Thunderskull's ship wasn't hovering directly above Keet, either. Governments tended to frown upon that sort of behaviour, especially when it came to heavily armed combat vessels. Xotl had been prepared to exit Nasako's atmosphere and perform a radar scan outside of orbit, but fortunately it hadn't come to that. The Xocha pilot spotted the pirate starship shortly after leaving Keet's airspace.

They'd spotted the large lake to the north of the city during their initial approach. Now, having seen how much wood was used in the settlement's ongoing construction, Xotl wondered whether the thin woodland flanking the lake on all sides had once been considerably more abundant. The still water shimmered a tranquil blue, punctuated only by the reflections of green canopies and wispy white clouds.

Oh, and an enormous pirate flagship.

Half a mile long and with a forward bow shaped like an iron cowcatcher, Thunderskull's pride and joy was an almighty leviathan of a dreadnought. Its dark grey hull was gnarly, sharp and twisted, like it had picked a fight with a minefield and come out the victor. All manner of ballistic turrets, las-beam pylons and missile launchers adorned its port and starboard flanks. And painted down those flanks in barely legible runes was its name...

The *Howling Rat*.

The flagship floated inert and lifeless. But Xotl spotted at least a dozen figures below, pitching tents and arranging supply crates. They were gearing up for something.

"Your hunch was correct," Xotl reported over the dashboard's comm unit. "Thunderskull's flagship is approximately ten klicks out from Keet. It looks as if his landing party has set up camp amongst the trees a couple of hundred metres from the lake."

"Dammit," Gecki replied, her voice crackling through the ship's speakers. "Good work, Xotl. Head back to the city before anyone spots you, yeah? We don't want Thunderskull knowing we're here."

"Understood," Xotl spluttered, only too eager to turn the *Silver Hart* around.

Sheni hated stairs. Skip drives could carry him from one end of the galaxy to the other in a matter of hours, but he still had to use his legs to move from a lower spot of ground to a high one? It was an absolute joke.

Gecki had insisted they climb to the highest point in the city before deciding what to do next. It would give them a better lay of the land, she said. Again, Sheni had argued that this was what the ship was for. It was as if Gecki didn't trust Xotl's report, or something. Needed to see Thunderskull's dreadnought for herself.

It was easy for Gecki. She had thighs like kebab spits. Sheni, on the other hand, had skipped leg day for the past five years. And he wasn't just dragging himself up the hill, either. Alan bounced along behind him like a sad party balloon that's lost half its helium. And as with a balloon, Sheni couldn't risk letting go of the green menace's hand in case he flew out of sight blowing a massive raspberry.

Stars above, his legs ached. His head ached, too. *And* he was hungry again. He wondered if the festival was still giving away free food...

"Couldn't we have discussed the job over a pint, or something?" he wheezed. "Or a cup of water, you know? I'm shrivelling up like a rotten apple over here."

"Quit your whining," she rasped. "If you can't walk up a hill, how can I trust you to evade capture while fleeing with someone's priceless heirloom?"

"If we do a job right, we shouldn't have to run at all. Can you take over watching Alan, at least? He's making my arm hurt."

Alan gurgled.

"Not my problem." Gecki shook her head. "You're the

one who insisted on bringing him along. Let him ride on your back, or whatever."

It wasn't a terrible suggestion. Alan seemed perfectly happy sitting on top of Sheni's shoulders, waving his favourite wrench in the air like an airport marshaller and dribbling affectionately at passersby. Carrying him didn't hurt his back, either. Alan weighed about as much as a house cat.

Sheni glanced further up the hill and groaned. The path winding its way up to the modest plateau at its peak seemed to stretch on forever. From the lookout point grew a half-ruined tower another forty metres tall. Sheni really hoped Gecki didn't consider it necessary to trudge up that as well.

A number of Nasakoans strolling down the other way smiled at him. He grinned back as best he could, assuming most were intrigued by Alan, but the closer they got to the top, the more forced his smiles became. Gecki had just killed someone. Sure, it was in self defence, but even so. Remaining out in public, it felt… reckless.

Anxiety gnawed away at his belly until he had to say something.

"Do you reckon Szaladar sounded the alarm? After he got back to his office, I mean."

"I would have thought so," Gecki replied. She didn't look back at him when she spoke. "There was a dead body in it."

"Yeah. I'm just wondering if hanging around one of the city's major landmarks is the smart move. In case they're looking for people matching our description, you know? The three of us kind of stand out."

"The altitude helps me think," she snarled dismissively.

"Funny," Sheni replied. "It just makes me light-headed."

"Hypobaric hypoxia," Alan mumbled innocently to himself.

Against Sheni's better judgement, they did eventually reach the top. Alan flung himself from Sheni's shoulders and raced off to explore the ruins before Sheni could stop him. Sheni sighed. He was too tired to give chase. Let the half-sentient booger fall to his death for all he cared. This whole heist was a bust. All Sheni wanted to do was crawl back inside the *Silver Hart* and disappear somewhere in the galaxy so crummy and remote even Slugbarrow couldn't find them.

Then he remembered the tracking device embedded in the ship's rear end.

Gods, they were so screwed.

He sat down beside Gecki on a long stone bench just behind the metal barrier that bordered the lookout point. A Nasakoan family sat together at the far end, talking loudly. Most of Keet was visible before them. A sprawling, ancient and surprisingly eclectic city of yellows and browns, shadows trickling from east to west with all the haste of honey. Rolling waves of houses, cresting and crashing down over one another. Crumbling palaces of clay; new towering developments on the outskirts built with sandstone bricks. And to their right, the port. A *real* port with sailboats and fishing ships and wooden jetties with coils of chunky rope. Gulls circled overhead. Every now and again one would dive into the frothing water like an arrow and emerge with a fish speared on its beak.

It was a beautiful view at sundown, he'd give her that.

"What is this, Gecki? One last evening together before we lose the ship and go our separate ways?"

Gecki snorted.

"What happened to Mr. Optimistic? I thought I was the one who needed to... how do you put it? Ah, yes... *lighten up*."

"Come on, you still think we can turn this job around? We're in a race against Thunderskull, for heaven's sake. He's got a bloodthirsty pirate crew working for him. We have a starfish and a simpleton."

"A small team can be more efficient," was Gecki's wry reply.

"Yes, well, a corpse branded with a pirate insignia just showed up in the High Priest's office. Even if the authorities haven't figured out we're after the krustallos egg, Szaladar will be under constant protection. It'll be next to impossible to get that medallion from his staff now. And even if we did, which we won't, you just know that stage is going to be crawling with guards armed to the teeth with electric pikes."

"Good. We'll want as much security guarding that egg as possible."

"*Will we?*" Sheni raised his eyebrows, flabbergasted. "Are you all right, Gecki? Thunderskull's goon didn't stab you in the brain, did he?"

Gecki smiled triumphantly. Her tongue licked away the strings of spittle forming pillars between her teeth as she unfolded the scrap of paper she had clutched in her hand.

"Read this."

Sheni straightened the page out. It was some kind of invoice. His translator chip struggled to interpret the alien writing.

"It's a bill from some kind of glass blowing company..." He shook his head. "Looks local, I guess? I don't get it."

Gecki fixed him with a piercing yellow stare and waited for realisation to sink in. Sheni's eyes widened.

"No way..." He studied the invoice again. "You're telling me the egg on that plinth is a *fake?*"

"I knew there was something off about it. No taaffeite crystal is *that* clear, especially one that's supposed to have a baby krustallos growing inside. And did you hear the noise it made when Alan tapped it with his wrench?"

"Sounded sharp like a wine glass, yeah. Stars above. And you don't think anyone else in Keet knows?"

Gecki shrugged.

"Maybe they *all* know. Deep down in their hearts, if not for actual fact. Maybe it's only us outsiders they're trying to fool."

"Gecki, what if there is no such thing as a krustallos egg? Plenty of cultures go through rituals for things they know aren't true anymore, you know, for the sake of tradition."

"The krustallos might be super rare, but it *is* a real creature." Gecki cracked an amused smile. "What's less certain is whether their eggs are actually made of crystal, or if that part's just a myth. Either way, the real one must be hidden away somewhere private, right? Hard to celebrate a hatching without a freakin' egg…"

"I guess. But if the real egg isn't made of taaffeite crystal, what's the point in stealing it?"

"Like I said, the krustallos are super rare. Even a regular egg might be enough to clear our debt, if Peggi can find a buyer."

Sheni looked over at the ruined tower. Alan stood in a crumbled opening about halfway up, gazing at the city laid out before him as if he were a benevolent ruler who, as a child, had been kicked in the head by the royal steed.

"Moot point, isn't it?" Sheni turned back to Gecki. "We still don't have the medallion, and the longer we wait, the sooner Thunderskull makes his move."

"Let him. He doesn't know the egg on that stage is a fake, does he? As for the medallion…" She shrugged. "Szaladar only got a fake egg made a couple of weeks ago, right? That tells us they didn't already have a forgery to hand. The High

Priest must be taking every precaution not to have his big moment messed up. But that old cradle thing they've got up on the stage is certainly no recent invention, which means in every Sunrise Celebration up until now, it's only ever held the real one. I guess what I'm trying to say," she concluded, scratching her scales, "is that there's only the one plinth, and the real egg ain't sitting on it. We won't need the medallion."

"And if you're wrong?"

"Every good plan leaves room for a little improvisation."

Sheni buried his head in his hands, but he was smiling.

"Man, I wish I could see the look on Thunderskull's face when his crew brings back a smashed-up chunk of glass. I assume you know where the real egg's being kept?"

"Not for sure. But I'd put credits on it still being in that Sunrise Temple of theirs. Too risky to move it across the city, and they'll need it close by for when it hatches."

Sheni's smile faltered slightly.

"The temple? The same heavily guarded one Thunderskull is about to steal from? Maybe you can camouflage yourself, but how the hell am I supposed to sneak past all that?"

Gecki snorted and pointed a claw at the Sunrise Temple, far across the city. The festival was still in full flow despite the approach of evening. Even all the way up at the lookout point, Sheni could faintly hear the music in the markets. Electric floodlights joined forces with the candles and oil lanterns, sweeping across the roasted sky. The front of the temple had been carved into the sheer face of an enormous granite and sandstone rock formation, much like the one they'd just spent an hour climbing.

"It's one of the oldest structures in Keet," she explained. "Most of the surrounding districts sprung up around it over the following century or two, and residents would have come for their weekly worship from all sides of the city. Course, this was back when the temple was still open to the public. The tunnels on that stage aren't the only ways in and out. There are plenty more passageways on the other side of that rock, even if nobody uses them anymore."

"Secret entrances and distracted guards." Sheni beamed. "I like the sound of this. When do we make our move?"

"Tonight." Gecki stood up from the bench and beckoned for Sheni to do the same. "If we start walking now, we should get there just in time."

CHAPTER
TEN

Night fell. Much of Keet was illuminated only by the flickering flames of lanterns hanging from hooks outside ground floor doorways. Shadows were deep; the quiet, crooked alleys grew quieter and crookeder still. The air was sweet with the sound of distant drunken glee.

Sheni, Gecki and Alan were crouching behind an old, brittle wall, waiting for the right moment. They would have preferred to drop Alan off at the ship before initiating the heist, but that would have required a significant detour they couldn't afford. Of course, Sheni had grumbled to himself while nursing his throbbing calves, if Gecki hadn't insisted on climbing up that freakin' monolith for the sake of some damn perspective...

A pair of fireworks exploded, seconds apart, above the stage half a kilometre away. The cloudless black sky was filled with red, yellow and green sparks falling like a snow flurry. The brief flashes provided a menacing snapshot of the giant purple nebula creeping across the Nasakoans' star system. Big cheers from the crowds.

"Space petals," Alan cooed.

Sheni slowly poked his head around the wall, sucked his teeth, then ducked back into cover before he could be spotted. Two guards stood to either side of a pitch-black cave. Neither so much as twitched when the fireworks went off.

"Still no movement," he whispered. "Should we try a different tunnel?"

"We don't have time to go secret entrance window shopping," Gecki replied. "Besides, they'll all be guarded like this one."

"So, what do you suggest we do?"

"I s'pose we could take them out."

"Take them out?" Sheni glared at her. "These guards work for the city. They're innocent. Well... innocent compared to us, at least. We can't go around killing people for a shiny egg!"

"Who said anything about killing people? We only have to render them unconscious. Perhaps you're right, though. We still have two more days before Slugbarrow expects his credits. We should hold off until tomorrow. Put together a distraction, or something."

"Hold on a second," Sheni said, raising an indignant finger. "There's no way we're backing out now. Thunderskull's crew could strike at any moment, and who's to say he won't figure out the egg's a fake too? We're so close, Gecki." He winked. "Have a little faith."

"Oh, gods." Gecki groaned. "I think I liked you better when you thought the galaxy was crashing down around your ears. What's *your* brilliant plan, then?"

"Erm, you know." He scratched the back of his neck. "Take them out, like you said. Remember the trick we pulled in Teegarden that one time?"

"Ah, the Drunk Tourist routine. Very apt." Gecki shuddered lightly as her scales changed colour to match the wall beside them. "Count to twenty while I get in position."

She scuttled out of cover, her pattern shifting as she travelled from stone to dirt to wooden post. Sheni could only follow her blurry outline for a short while before he lost sight of her. He waited for fifteen seconds and then turned to Alan.

"Stay here until I call you," he said sternly.

Alan gurgled, hopefully in the affirmative.

Sheni flexed his shoulders, grimaced at the way his joints crunched, and then stumbled out from behind the wall, brow raised and blinking heavily.

The two guards paid him no attention at first. There were plenty of inebriated individuals at the festival, after all, though admittedly rather few on this side of the rock formation. He staggered towards them, his arms raised slightly for balance.

They bristled as he got closer. He sniffed heavily, as if the alcohol had made him congested, and puffed out his cheeks. Gods, this had better work. Those pikes of theirs looked like they could stab just as well as they could electrocute.

"Hey, excuse me," he mumbled. "I think I'm... *oof*. Sorry. Almost a bit sick, there. I think I'm lost. Can you point me in the direction of the erm... the..."

"The festival?" one of the guards said, glancing uneasily at his colleague.

"Yes! *Yesh*. That's the one." He stumbled forwards again, trying not to make eye contact for too long, swallowing hard like he was on the verge of throwing up. "Where is it?"

The guard closest to Sheni stepped away from his post

beside the cave, just far enough forward to point down the long, deserted road to Sheni's right. Behind him, the dark grey stone shimmered almost imperceptibly.

"A short walk that way. Just follow the music."

Sheni grinned and clapped his hands together. The two guards flinched and tightened their grips on their pikes for a moment, but that moment was fleeting. Sheni's smile was contagious.

"Thank you, gentlemen," he said, slurring his words a little extra as he spun around. "I shall be on my way."

"Maybe you should head home, spacer." Another glance between the guards, this one more bemused than concerned. "Consider sleeping this one off."

Sheni stopped and pointed a wandering finger back at the guard who'd shown him the way to the festival.

"Maybe *you* should sleep it off," he said, snorting.

All three of them laughed for a short moment, until the guard in question realised he didn't understand what was funny.

"Wait... what?"

Sheni punched him square in the face. Nasakoans weren't an especially hardy species, and the guard crashed to the floor like a crawfish in a copper diving suit. Sheni kicked his pike away. At the same time, Gecki dropped down from the rock face behind them and grabbed the second guard in a headlock, her scales reverting to their usual mint-green colour. He writhed about and scratched fruitlessly at her arm for a bit, then passed out.

Sheni's guard wasn't so fortunate. The guy was groaning and clumsily propping himself up on his elbows. If he cried out for help...

Alan thumped him on the head with his wrench. The

guard's eyes rolled back into his skull and he went limp. Sheni checked the guy's pulse and relaxed slightly. Still breathing.

"I thought I told you to wait," he hissed at Alan.

Alan smiled and dribbled unapologetically.

"Drag them inside and tie them up," Gecki snarled, "before anyone sees!"

Sheni grabbed the knocked-out guard by the feet and pulled him into the darkness of the cave mouth. He was heavier than Sheni expected, thanks to his bronze armour plates. He propped him up against the rock wall – he wouldn't want the poor guy to wake up with a stiff neck, you know – wrapped some rope around his wrists and gagged him with an old handkerchief, and then went back for his pike. Gecki was switching the other pike on and off. Its lightning bolts lit up the cave a pale blue.

"Reckon we should take them?" Gecki asked, sporting a mischievous grin.

"Nah." Sheni shook his head. "Subduing these guys was bad enough. Taking their weapons invites conflict. We're thieves, not savage pirates like Thunderskull."

"Suit yourself."

Gecki shrugged, but she put down her pike all the same. Alan pottered off into the darkness. Sheni hesitated.

"I do feel sorry for these guys. Everyone's gonna blame them for the egg getting stolen."

"You don't know that. Besides, your guard's gonna wake up with one hell of a bruised jaw. He can tell people he bravely fought you off."

"Yeah, maybe."

"Come on." Gecki grabbed him by the arm. "Glory and riches await."

The cave narrowed into a tunnel, where they came to an iron door that could only have been a few decades old at most. Gecki unlocked it with a set of keys she stole from the guards outside. Sheni could barely walk down the tunnel's length without hunching over. It would have been impossible to see anything were it not for the strange bioluminescent toadstools sprouting up from between subterranean roots along the path. He wondered if this tunnel had been carved by the Nasakoan people millennia ago, or if it had been shaped by natural phenomena long forgotten by the rest of Keet's landscape. Perhaps harsh rivers had once run down to the shore.

Within a murky minute they entered a wider chamber, its walls adorned with stone carvings. Faces, aghast. Pottery. More winged beasts like the one adorning the High Priest's medallion. Many were too eroded or shrouded in cobwebs to recognise.

Alan waited patiently for them to catch up. He was staring at the various carvings with glassy intrigue in his bulging eyes.

Sheni suddenly stuck out his arm to impede Gecki's progress.

"Wait a moment. Something's not right..."

The ground was covered in flat, misshapen and yet carefully arranged stones. Some stuck up from the chamber's floor more than others.

"Those tiles," he said, each word dragged out to twice its usual length. "They look odd to you?"

Gechi squatted down on her haunches, squinted, and blew dust from the floor.

"Yeah, like some of them don't sit in the ground quite right. You reckon...?"

"Pressure switches." Sheni nodded. "A trap to keep out

people like us. Maybe if we look for something heavy, we can trigger them from a distance..."

They searched the tunnel behind them for large stones. Alan measured himself against the closest carving, babbled something incoherent, and then sprinted forwards. Sheni tried to grab him, but it was too late.

"Alan, no!"

The little green marble may have weighed less than a pouch of gold coins, but it was still enough to depress every tile in his way. A heavy *clunk* rumbled beneath their feet. Arrows shot out from holes in the various stone faces and mythical creatures. They whooshed mere millimetres above Alan's domed torso and shattered harmlessly against the stone walls to either side.

"Good gods," Gecki groaned, her scales a lighter, sickly shade of green.

Alan arrived at the other end and turned to face them. His incessant smile fell slightly, as if he were disappointed they hadn't followed, and he took a step back in their direction.

"No, stay where you—" Sheni ran a hand through his hair. "Stars above..."

Alan sprinted back across the stones, arms held out for a hug. Nothing happened. Once Sheni had a tight grip on the suicidal jelly bean, Gecki stretched out her leg and tapped the nearest tile with a trepidatious toe-claw.

"Seems clear," she said, shrugging.

Even so, Sheni elected to crawl his way across on his hands and knees, just in case. Sod's law dictated he'd step on the one tile Alan had managed to miss. Gecki rolled her eyes and strolled behind him patiently.

"Now we know why they guard the entrances," Sheni mused, standing up straight upon reaching the other side.

"It's not to stop the locals from getting into the temple. It's to keep them from getting killed by their own ancestors' traps…"

"Concentrate on where you're stepping," she rasped. "I'm taller than you, and I'm not getting decapitated here. My head's the only part of me that doesn't grow back."

Sheni stepped as slowly and carefully as possible, scrutinising every suspicious patch of dirt. But there were no more traps along the tunnel ahead, just a disappointingly abrupt end to their narrow cave.

"This can't be it," Gecki growled, checking back the way they came. "What's the point of this godsdamn tunnel if *this* is all it leads to?"

"We have to be missing something." Sheni brushed his hand against the sheer wall at the tunnel's end. "Look. Something's carved into the stone here. Runes."

Gecki helped him clear the wall of dust and grime while Alan swung his wrench around with two hands as if it were a broadsword.

"I come and go but once a day," Sheni said, slowly reading the passage aloud. "Reflect on me to light your way. What's that supposed to mean?"

"Are you kidding? The answer's obviously the sun. Gods, people were easy to fool back then."

"Well, I don't *see* any sun," he said, peering around the gloomy tunnel. He found a small hole hidden amongst the riddle's runes, tried peering through it, and then jolted upright as he was struck by an idea. "Mirrors! I bet they bounced light all the way down from the entrance using mirrors!"

"What, like these things?" Gecki irritably flicked the dull sheet of tin by her head with a claw. "I think their reflecting days are over."

"Of *course* they're broken." Sheni sighed. "They've been here for centuries. Well, let's see if we can get them aligned anyway."

"It wouldn't matter even if the mirrors were freakin' spotless," Gecki snarled. "It's the dead of night, you idiot! Where are you getting any sun from?"

"Damn it. Those guards will wake up long before dawn, I reckon..."

Gecki glared at him in furious disbelief.

"And the mirrors will *still* be broken!"

Alan waddled up to Sheni and tugged at the pocket of his jacket containing his data pad.

"Stop it, Alan. We don't have time to watch *Gordo & Friends* right now."

Alan tugged harder.

"Specious lumens," he said insistently.

"I don't know if that's an episode title, or..." He paused, then brandished the data pad at Gecki. "The flashlight on my data pad. I don't know why I didn't think of this before!"

"Because it's hardly a sun, is it?"

"No, but it's a form of concentrated light, you know? I doubt the original riddle masters anticipated we'd carry tiny stars around in our pockets one day, but here we are. Now, maybe if I line it up just right..."

He angled the data pad so it matched the mirror and shone its flashlight at the hole in the wall. It didn't work. Gecki huffed. Ignoring her, Sheni wrapped a finger around the diode, and slowly curled it tighter to block out more and more of the light...

When only the tiniest sliver of his torch pierced the hole, the chamber shuddered hard enough to shake fragments of rock loose from the ceiling, and the entire wall rolled to one side with an earthy crash. Sheni jumped back. Gecki smirked in sharp-toothed amazement.

"Well, butter my scales and call me a brisket. We're in."

Sheni grinned, pocketed his data pad, and extended a chivalrous hand towards the temple.

"Ladies first…"

CHAPTER ELEVEN

Sheni kept a tight hand on Alan in case other traps or riddles lay ahead. More carvings lined the craggy walls to either side of their dark tunnel, but none possessed any suspicious holes that he could see, and he had a feeling the caverns were growing slowly brighter.

Crackling. Pops. It sounded like a fire. He glanced at Gecki, who nodded. They hunched over in unison and hugged the wall of the tunnel as they approached its corner. Even Alan, who couldn't get much closer to the ground if he tried, and whose smile certainly couldn't stretch much wider, took long, exaggeratedly cautious steps.

"Wait," Sheni whispered, raising his hand.

He heard scratching on the rocks to their right. Slowly turning his stiff neck, his heart hammering in his chest, he spotted a small, six-legged lizard watching them with bulbous eyes that blinked sideways. It tilted its head at them curiously before scurrying out of sight.

Sheni let out a sigh of relief, ignored the exasperated expression he imagined Gecki was making behind his back, and led their group around the corner.

It was a fire he'd heard. A pretty big one, too. A cast-iron brazier, a good five feet in diameter, stood just outside the exit of the tunnel. The wooden logs piled inside burned an angry red colour. The heat made Sheni wince and shield his face while Gecki slithered close.

"Be careful," he whispered, as his eyes struggled to adjust to the sudden brightness. "We're not skulking in the shadows anymore. Someone might see us."

Gecki's scales shimmered a fiery red.

"Someone might see *you*, maybe."

Sheni retreated back to a shaded spot close to where they'd seen the lizard. The brazier was installed on an elevated ridge that overlooked a much larger subterranean hall. Other braziers, all burning with the same colour and ferocity, illuminated other ridges and balconies as well as the floor of the cavern. Enormous red statues of ancient Nasakoan priests, carved out of the rocky monolith itself, stood around the hall, facing inwards.

He ducked down as he spotted an armoured Nasakoan patrolling the coarse path on the far side of the hall. Alan remained inches from the brazier, the reflections of its flames flickering in his big, watery eyes, so Sheni hurriedly yanked him into cover, too. Gecki was nowhere to be seen.

"I count six guards," she hissed from her position up on the rock face beside him.

"How many times..." Sheni shuddered. "I've asked you not to do that, Gecki. How do you want to handle them?"

"We could knock them all out, one by one," she suggested. "But the cavern's too well lit. They'd figure out they were being picked off pretty quickly."

Picked off. Sheni raised an eyebrow. It was hard to tell, sometimes, just how violent Gecki was willing to be. Too many years spent fighting to survive on the fringes, he reckoned. He hoped he never ended up that cutthroat. Or that bitter.

"I think we'd be better off trying to avoid them entirely," he replied. "At least until we're close to the egg, you know?"

"And where *is* the egg, huh? You're the one who wanted to rush in here. Another day of brainstorming and we could have plotted out a map of this place."

"Hey! Sneaking in through an old passageway was *your* plan, so quit acting like I should know my way around!"

"You'd be sulking aboard the *Silver Hart* right now if it weren't for me finding that invoice," she hissed. "Poor Sheni, counting down the hours till we have to hand the ship over to Slugbarrow thanks to *his* screw-ups. Don't you—"

Alan whacked each of them on the head with his wrench, then dribbled sedately. Sheni rubbed his skull. That was gonna leave a lump.

"Alan's right," he whispered. "This isn't getting us anywhere. Nobody knows we're here, right? We have the advantage. So I say we just stick to the shadows. This place can't be too big, you know? Sooner or later, we'll find it."

"Good enough for me." Gecki nodded and dropped down from the rock. There was a slight dissonance as her scales took a moment adapting to the change in background. "Now we just need to work out which way is which..."

"I thought you had a good sense of direction? Better than mine, at any rate."

"Not underground, I don't." Her upper lip rolled back from her teeth. "Those traps threw me right off."

Somebody down below shouted, and all the guards snapped to attention. Sheni and Gecki ducked even further into cover. His blood ran as cold as hers. Were they rumbled? Had somebody discovered the two unconscious guards they'd hidden just inside the cave mouth? If so, they were trapped. No escaping the way they came.

But rather than secure the chamber, all six of the guards stationed inside it left their posts and sprinted out through a passageway on the far side of the room.

"What's got them all riled up?" Sheni asked.

"Thunderskull," Gecki replied, both her yellow and milky eyes widening. "Listen."

Sheni strained his ears. Humans weren't the best species when it came to hearing, but even he could make out the distant screams where there should have been joyous cheers.

"Xotl said Thunderskull's crew was gearing up for something," she continued. "They must be stealing the fake egg from the stage as we speak."

"Then we'd better get a move on. Gods, I hope they don't hurt anyone. Badly, I mean," he added, remembering the punch he'd delivered to that poor Nasakoan's jaw.

He nudged Gecki in the ribs as they sidled past the brazier.

"Hey. Good thing we didn't wait another day, you know?"

Gecki grumbled and shoved him forward.

They knew which way they *shouldn't* go. That was obvious from the moment every guard in the chamber had sprinted out in the direction of the stage. And if the public-facing side of the temple was in that direction, it made sense that anything valuable – say, a rare and priceless krustallos egg made of pure taaffeite crystal – would be safely stashed the other way.

Of course, what with the tunnels having probably been formed naturally hundreds of millennia ago, figuring out how to head the other way wasn't always as simple as it seemed...

"We're back in the main chamber again," Gecki hissed. "Gods, we don't have time for this!"

Sheni swore as he exited the tunnel behind her. She was right. This was the second passageway they'd tried, and both had led them around in a loop. He didn't recall them passing any forks in the path, but then again, it had been lit only by drooping candles and anaemic toadstools...

He held him breath and listened. Yep. Laser fire still screeched back and forth outside. Thunderskull's crew was wreaking havoc out there. And all for a two week-old lump of glass.

Should they have warned Keet about Thunderskull? Sheni clenched his jaw. That would have meant giving up any hope of stealing the egg for themselves. Probably would have meant losing the *Silver Hart*, too. But all those innocent festival-goers caught in the crossfire...

"Stop daydreaming." Gecki smacked him in the back. "Which tunnel did we just try?"

"Erm..." He studied all of the entrances around the ground floor and the surrounding ridges. "That one, maybe? No, that's the one we arrived through..."

"Gah! This is stupid. We should have grabbed one of the guards, forced them to show us where the egg is. We'll never find it without a map."

Sheni paced down the ridge, scratching at the three day old stubble carpeting his chin. Think, Sheni, think. If you were a sparkly egg that needed keeping from absolutely everyone, where would you be?

He peered around the back of one of the huge statues looming over the central pit and clicked his fingers.

"Up there. I know for a fact we haven't tried *that* one."

A balcony had been carved out of the rear rock face, much higher than all the rest. Smaller statues stood to either side of the alcove. The tunnel behind glowed brightly.

"The question is," he said, hands on hips, "how do we get up there?"

Gecki bared her teeth and shrugged.

"The same way you get up any rock wall. You climb it."

"What about Alan? He's got arms like shoelaces."

"That's what these are for," she said, patting his shoulder. "What is he if not a sentient backpack?"

Sheni wasn't really worried about Alan's upper body strength. If Alan wanted to get up somewhere inconvenient, he never failed to find a way. It was Sheni's own ability to ascend vertical terrain that concerned him. Especially now, with the added – albeit minuscule – weight of Alan on his shoulders.

Gecki crawled up the rocks with all the difficulty of plucking something off a high shelf. Sheni took one look at the wall and groaned. He wasn't afraid of heights. But he *was* afraid of hitting the ground hard and fast enough to not get back up again.

"Come on, Alan." He picked him up and held him against his shoulders until he latched on. "Try not to dribble down my back, all right?"

Alan gurgled inconclusively.

Holding onto the closest statue for dear life, Sheni extended one foot out over the edge until he found somewhere robust to put it. Then he reached for a suitable handhold and pulled his whole body across. His fingers already ached. The bottom of his stomach felt like it had dropped to somewhere around his knees.

He reckoned it was a six metre fall to the chamber floor. Already enough to break something important, and he'd need to climb another half a dozen metres more to reach the balcony. He swallowed hard and chewed his bottom lip. Get a grip, Sheni. You've gone toe-to-toe with Prymalis attack ships. This isn't how heroes are supposed to behave...

It wasn't as bad as he thought. Easier than most climbing walls, probably, because of how damn lumpy and irregular the rock face was. He really had to dig his fingers into any crevasses he found, and he wished his hands weren't so freakin' slippery with sweat, but his boots had good grip. When he glanced up, Gecki was already lounging on the edge of the stone platform, tapping her claws against the cold, hard floor.

Her weary face grew serious.

"Hurry up. Climb faster."

"Not all of us have Velcro for hands, you know?"

"I'm being serious, human. I can hear people coming back."

Sheni shot a look over his shoulder and was hit by a wave of vertigo. Nobody had emerged from the tunnels on the ground floor of the chamber... yet.

"Guards, or pirates?" he whispered desperately.

"How the stars should I know?" she rasped, reaching down to him. "You're the one with ears on the outside of your head. Climb!"

Sheni scrambled up the rocks as best he could, bashing his knees and scraping his shins against the jagged stone. Could he hear the sound of footsteps, or was he just imagining it now Gecki had put the idea in his head? All he knew was his blood was pounding in his temples so hard his vision had started to shake.

He reached for the next handhold up.

His foot slipped.

A scaly hand shot down and grabbed his arm before he could tumble more than a few inches toward his death. Alan's hands tightened around his throat, but he let out a happy giggle. Oh, good. Sheni was glad *someone* was having a fun time. With Gecki doing most of the heavy lifting, he managed to climb the last three feet of the wall and roll safely onto the floor of the alcove.

"No time to rest," Gecki rasped, pulling him upright. "Gotta move."

They hurried into the alcove. Sheni felt some relief, at least; whoever was coming down that tunnel towards the chamber wasn't likely to follow them upstairs any time soon. Not unless they could scale walls like Gecki. They passed lit candles in slender nooks chiseled out of the rock, and then flaming torches nestled in iron brackets further on.

"We never did find out where the High Priest sleeps at night, did we?" Sheni whispered.

"Or where he'd go if his temple got attacked," Gecki replied. "Step quietly. We may not be alone up here, either."

The alcove quickly took them to a cramped room stuffed full of tatty banners and unsorted trinkets. Cubbies of dusty scrolls. Stone tablets etched with forgotten runes. Fragments of petrified wood. Chalices as gold as Szaladar's sceptre. Sheni didn't know how valuable these artefacts would be to somebody outside of Nasakoan culture, but he suspected there was more than enough there to pay off the crew's debts.

His debts, he reminded himself.

"Relics," Gecki said with a satisfied snarl. "I think we're close."

"Let's just grab the egg and get out of here," Sheni said with a sigh. "This is hardly the heist we signed up for."

"But it is one that'll keep a hull over our heads for the next cycle. You did good, human."

Sheni bristled. You did good *for* a human, is what she really meant. And truth be told, he didn't feel good about any of this. He didn't feel good *at all*.

A narrow staircase cut into the rock. Back down they went, slowly creeping counter-clockwise, descending deeper and deeper still, until they arrived unceremoniously at a small door. Its hinges were black and rusted; its dark wood was gnarly and warped, barely fitting the frame.

It was the first door they'd encountered since solving that stupid riddle, even if it was one hard knock away from splintering in half. Sheni was sure something important had to be stashed behind it.

With the claws of one hand raised to strike, Gecki slowly creaked the door open.

Wherever they were in the rock formation, it was dingy and unguarded. Gecki and Sheni both stooped down to fit through the doorway. A dank cave awaited them. Water trickled from a crevasse into a turgid rock pool in the corner. Oil lanterns were balanced precariously on some of the boulders around its periphery. Looking up, Sheni was surprised to discover not a ceiling of stone overhead, but of stars. A rough, vertical shaft bored through the centre of the monolith.

He lowered his eyes and found himself face to face with a giant, grey dragon, seemingly asleep.

"Stars above," he gasped, clutching his chest. "That damn statue almost put me in the ground."

Gecki scraped a claw along the dragon's brittle flank.

"I don't think that's a statue," she said, giving the grit under her claw a suspicious sniff. "That there's calcified skin. I think we're looking at the old krustallos."

Sheni took a nervous step backwards.

"The dead one, right?"

"She's in a pretty bad state if she ain't. Has to be, anyway. A krustallos only lays a single egg in her lifetime, and always right as she's about to die. Or so the story goes."

Sheni placed a trembling hand on the beast's head. She was enormous. Thirty foot in length, maybe more. It was hard to tell for certain, what with her passing away while curled up like a giant, scaly pussycat. A pair of wings lay folded across her back.

Alan had, of course, interpreted the krustallos corpse as a climbing frame. He stood on the ridges of its spine and frantically waved his wrench in the air.

"I think someone's found the prize," Sheni said, grinning for the first time since he solved the riddle.

They hurried down to the excitable green kidney bean, hearts pounding, heads buzzing. There, nestled amongst her talons, was the krustallos egg. The *real* egg, not some fake glass sculpture. Its shell was thick, utterly opaque, and sparkled with flecks of blue and green.

Gecki gently plucked it from the dead krustallos's grasp and held it up to the starlight.

"Now, *this* egg..." She salivated with desire. "*This* egg is shiny."

She clutched it to her chest as half a dozen leather-clad pirates suddenly poured in from the surrounding tunnels. The cave glistened with chrome teeth.

"More accurately," Thunderskull said, marching into the chamber behind them, "that egg is *mine*."

CHAPTER TWELVE

Thunderskull stuck out his three fingered hand.

"Egg. Now."

Sheni took a step backward. His ankle bashed into the rigid claw of the dead krustallos. Alan hopped down the calcified corpse to join him. Gecki remained where she stood, her arms clutching the egg as if she'd laid it herself, snarling at the rival pirate captain.

"You know the code," she rasped. "We found it first."

"And now I'm stealing it off you," Thunderskull explained, pulling a revolver from his holster. "Screw the code. Hand it over."

Even amongst pirates, Thunderskull struck an imposing figure. His head looked like the skull on the old Jolly Roger flags, bone white and covered in keratin. He was a Calcurian, a stocky humanoid species who were barely tolerant enough of other races to join the wider galactic coalition known as the Ministerium of Cultured Planets. In stark contrast to the menagerie of dishevelled, threadbare pirates fanning out around him, Thunderskull wore a fitted uniform of black leather and spiky steel armour plating.

Sheni wondered how long it had taken Thunderskull to find a victim with the exact right measurements.

Creeping out behind Thunderskull, hunched over like a dog flinching from a boot, came Two-Toe Tim. Dark bags hung under his eyes. The man clearly hadn't slept since they spoke. Sheni glared daggers at him. Two-Toes gave an apologetic shrug as if to say, *You turned down my offer. What else did you expect me to do?*

"No." Gecki bared her teeth. "We *need* this."

Thunderhead smiled, nonplussed.

"Suit yourself."

He shot Gecki in the arm. She yelped and dropped the egg. It hit the floor with a loud thump, but didn't break. If anything, Sheni reckoned it was the stone which cracked.

He ignored the egg and rushed to Gecki. Her left arm hung limp by her side. She took a long, painful hiss of breath.

"Stars above," he said, horrified, his eyes flitting between her and Thunderskull. "Gecki, are you all right?"

"I'm fine," she rasped, blood seeping through her claws. "It'll heal if I pick out the bullet."

Sheni swore and marched forward. Thunderskull swung his gun around and aimed it at him instead.

"Will *you* heal, human?"

Sheni backed off, hands raised.

"Two-Toes, you worm," Thunderskull shouted over his shoulder. "Get the egg. Make sure it's the real one."

Two-Toes scurried out and strained to lift the krustallos egg into his arms. It was evidently heavier than Gecki made it look.

"What the hell are you doing?" Sheni whispered. "I told you not to get mixed up with pirates like Thunderskull. You know you won't last a week, right?"

"You didn't exactly leave me with much choice," he hissed back. "And if *you* hadn't stolen *my* idea, neither of us would be in this mess."

Two-Toes shuffled back over to Thunderskull and inspected the egg with a retractable eye-piece.

"Looks like taaffeite crystal to me," he said with a sheepish grin.

"The worm done good," Thunderskull announced to his crew. They sniggered and cheered. "We'll make a pirate out of you yet."

Sheni clenched his jaw. Two-Toes made eye contact with him and his hopeful smile quickly vanished.

"When did you figure out the real egg was kept hidden away?" Sheni asked Thunderskull. "Was it before or after you started slaughtering people?"

"Nah, I knew it was a fake as soon as I got here. That glass bauble might have the locals fooled, but not me."

"Then why the hell'd you attack the stage?"

"Distraction." Thunderskull scoffed. "What? You didn't think I dragged all the guards outside for your sake, did you?"

"You sacrificed members of your own crew," Gecki said, appalled.

"Eh, a few. Can't have been worth much if they got taken out by a bunch of villagers, though, right?" Thunderskull wrapped an arm around a trembling Two-Toe Tim. "Besides. Always more fodder ready to sign up."

"You're a psychopath," Sheni mumbled.

"I'm a captain who isn't about to lose his ship," Thunderskull replied. "That being said…"

He gestured with his gun for Gecki to come join him.

"You killed my first mate, lizard. Qorgin was worth

double anyone else in my crew. Which means you're coming with me."

"Like hell she is," Sheni yelled. Alan raised his wrench above his head defiantly.

"Qorgin tried to kill me first," Gecki snarled.

"I'd have expected nothing less. Violent guy. You still owe me."

"Just take the egg," Sheni said with a pleading sigh.

"Already got the egg." Thunderskull shrugged. "I can make even more credits by taking her."

Gecki took a step forward, still clasping her wounded arm.

"It's all right," she growled at Sheni when he went to protest. "I can handle myself. Just make sure Alan and Xotl get out okay."

She stalked over to Thunderskull. Gecki stood a good foot taller than him, but he never dropped his cocky smirk. She probably could have torn his head off had she not been injured, but they were surrounded by raiders with rifles. Even a hint of violence would get them all killed.

"I'll come with you," she grumbled, saliva dripping from her canines, "but you leave the rest of my crew alone."

Everyone glanced up as the underside of a *Howling Rat* support skiff chugged into view above the vertical shaft, blocking out the starlight. Its white hover-thrusters throbbed. A forest of ropes whipped down the shaft like jungle vines and coiled on the floor between Sheni and the pirates.

"Fine by me," Thunderskull replied cordially. "Somebody's gotta take the fall for this."

He clipped himself onto one of the ropes. The other pirates, including Two-Toe Tim, did the same. One of

Thunderskull's goons scooped the egg into a black sack, while another was assigned to Gecki.

Thunderskull gave his rope a sharp tug. He ran his tongue over his teeth as he began to ascend.

"I wouldn't hang around, if I were you," he called down to Sheni and Alan. "The locals are gonna be *pissed*."

His cronies laughed as they disappeared up the shaft behind him. Two-Toes gave Sheni another apologetic look before he left. Gecki refused to make eye contact, her lips curled back at the sides. Sheni couldn't tell if she was furious with him or simply resigned to her fate.

With everyone else gone from the cave, the quake of furious footsteps could be felt – heard, even – through the rock. Ripples echoed across the rock pool. Sheni raced back to the door and latched it shut.

Alan was standing under the shaft, his big eyes glistening as he stared blankly at the departing skiff. Sheni grabbed his hand on his way toward the tunnels.

"She ain't coming back, buddy," he said. "I'm afraid it's just you and me."

CHAPTER THIRTEEN

All of the tunnels looked the same. Was he looping back on himself, headed right toward the Nasakoan guards hunting him? Everything was so twisty-turney. He could still hear their pursuit, their angry boots and seething shouts flowing past him through the labyrinth, as likely from ahead as behind, above as below...

Sheni still had Alan's hand grasped tightly in his own. He couldn't risk the little guy running the opposite way down any fork they came across, or worse still, stopping to stand and dribble serenely beside a particularly luminescent toadstool. He didn't know what the punishment for stealing a krustallos egg was in Keet, or how they'd prove it was him given the, you know, *lack of evidence*, but he didn't intend for either him or Alan to find out.

He didn't hold a lot of faith in any of the galaxy's justice systems, let alone one belonging to a backwater court of distraught locals. But his faith in a bunch of foiled guards wielding sharpened pikes capable of slicing him into char-grilled chicken strips? Even weaker.

"How is it so hard to put up some damn signs?" he muttered to himself, frantically choosing one dark passageway over another without rhyme or reason.

But how much safer would he be once they got out of the temple? Alan was a shamrock bowling ball; he was a six foot human. Neither of them exactly blended in with a short, tentacle-faced population.

Whereas Thunderskull, Two-Toes and Gecki were probably already out of the city by now, blasting across the barren plains on their skiff, headed for the pirate captain's mechanised flagship.

Gecki. She was gone, stolen from him just like the egg. What a sorry mess this was. He hadn't been apart from Gecki – not *really*, not in any meaningful way – since the day she'd rescued him from that raider-infested rock on which he'd been stranded. The *Silver Hart* was her ship, not his. He owed her his life, always would.

And now she was Thunderskull's prisoner. His latest treasure. A play thing, perhaps. Gods...

He shivered as the skin on the back of his neck grew taut. Gecki would have known what to do in this situation. She usually kept a cool head. Either that, or she tore off somebody else's.

Sheni reached the end of their present passageway. At first he believed it to be a dead end, an assumption reinforced when Alan sprinted face-first into the wall of pebbles, dirt and twisted roots. But then he noticed the crack between two partially collapsed rock walls. There were stone archways, tiles and statues on the other side, plus a hell of a lot of cobwebs that draped over everything like wedding veils.

More importantly, there were footprints in the dust. Thunderskull's men had come through here.

This was their way out.

Alan tugged at Sheni's hand as he squeezed through the gap.

"Parietal apportion," he gurgled.

"Honestly, Alan, I wish for once you'd just—"

Sheni jerked backward as two curved blades swung out from the archways and passed millimetres from his face and abdomen. A freshly trimmed strand of hair floated past his eyes.

Without moving his head, he carefully peered down at Alan, who hiccupped.

"Chop chop."

"Stars above." Sheni gritted his teeth hard enough to make his head shake. "Did Thunderskull reset the traps as he went, or something?"

Alan pulled him across the tiles with great urgency. Sheni flinched and ducked, but the trap didn't trigger again. Perhaps it needed time to reset. He closed his eyes and let Alan guide him down the rest of the tiled pathway, fully expecting to receive a whip trap's worth of spikes in his gut at any moment, but no stone so much as clicked underfoot.

When he opened his eyes again, something orange glowed around the next corner. He yanked Alan backward, momentarily making him resemble an inflatable space hopper as he sailed brainlessly through the air in reverse, and they crept more carefully toward the light together.

"You have got to be kidding me," Sheni hissed.

They were back in the main chamber again.

Alan tried to wander off. Sheni pulled him back into cover. Gods, this was the worst place to be! All he could hear was the crackle of the brazier next to him. After five minutes spent sprinting through gloomy tunnels, its bright flames made it irritatingly hard to see, too.

Damn the stars. He counted four armoured Nasakoans patrolling the chamber. Maybe five; he might have lost count when one disappeared into the tunnels they were guarding. Three were down on the ground floor, making sure the thief didn't escape through the stage exit. The other was making a patrol of the ridge that ran behind the giant statues, inspecting each passage with the glow of his electro-pike. Right now the guy was on the far side to Sheni, but Sheni suspected he had less than thirty seconds to go before he was rumbled.

He squinted and scrutinised every tunnel around the elevated edge. Which was the one Gecki had first led them down, the one with the sunlight riddle? They all looked as craggy and hole-like as each other...

"Karst," Alan cooed.

"Shut it, Alan!"

There, over on his right. He was ninety percent sure that was the one. Eighty percent, maybe. With the lone guard patrolling the ridge already a quarter of the way around since Sheni first clocked him, those odds would have to do.

"Please, Alan. Keep your head down and your mouth shut, all right?"

Alan smiled. The eye not looking directly at Sheni slowly squelched sideways.

Well, at least his head was always low, Sheni supposed.

They hurried around the edge, away from the guard. Sheni, hunched over double, ensured they remained in the shadows outside of the braziers' reach whenever possible. A nervous smile crept onto Sheni's face. They were doing this. They were getting out. Gecki's secret entrance was only a stone's throw away...

Something considerably harder and faster than a stone suddenly buried itself in the cave wall beside his head.

Sheni ducked into cover behind the nearest brazier with Alan in tow. More projectiles pinged off its old, iron bowl.

"They have guns," he mumbled to Alan. "Of *course* they have guns. Everybody in the galaxy does. Ridiculous assumption to make, that they wouldn't have guns just because they've got big spiky sticks as well. I told Gecki we shouldn't have sold our stunners, you know, but did she listen…?"

He waited for a break in the barrage and then stood up from behind the brazier with his arms raised.

"Wait!"

All of the guards obeyed his instruction, even the one rushing around the ridge behind him, though they each had the good sense to look at least marginally confused by it. Sheni froze. Huh. He hadn't anticipated that. There wasn't really a precedent for what came next. *Wait* was just something you shouted right before the end.

"Sorry," he said, flashing them an apologetic smile as he shoved the brazier over.

The ancient bowl tipped easily, balanced as it was on the very lip of the ridge, and a calamity of red-hot coals and ash went showering into the pit below. The three guards on the ground floor scattered in a panic. One was almost immediately buried under an avalanche of cinders. Another tripped up trying to escape and face-planted the dirt. The third disappeared into one of the myriad tunnels he was guarding without so much a single glance back in Sheni's direction.

Not that Sheni hung about to check on their wellbeing. They'd be fine – what good was all their shiny armour otherwise, if it couldn't handle a little bit of heat? But he wouldn't be, not if they took many more shots at him. And as that thought crossed Sheni's mind, another tiny bullet almost travelled through it. He'd forgotten all about the Nasakoan chasing him around the ridge.

The exit was close. He was another second or two away from disappearing down its narrow crevasses, when he realised his hands were strangely empty...

Alan. His stomach shrivelled and he almost stopped running. Where the hell was Alan?

But then he spotted the little guy, right by the exit he was sprinting toward. How the weirdo had got there before him, Sheni had no idea. The bigger question was: why was Alan slowly walking backward?

Yet another well-armoured Nasakoan came wandering into the chamber. This one was rubbing his tentacled jaw and stumbling about like he was nursing a hangover. Ropes dangled from his wrists. Sheni inwardly winced. He recognised him as the guard he knocked unconscious outside. He blinked heavily as Sheni barrelled towards him, and his pained grimace turned into a scowl.

"I really am sorry," Sheni insisted, shoving the poor guy over the side of the ridge. "One day you'll look back at this and laugh!"

He scooped Alan up in his arms and sprinted down the tunnel, past the stone riddle-wall, over the arrow-spitting trap tiles, through darkened corridors of rock and out into the fledgling dawn beyond.

Good riddance, he thought. He didn't want to see another ancient temple for as long as he breathed, which admittedly might not be all that substantial a length of time.

Because now he needed to escape a city hell-bent on putting his head where the egg ought to be.

CHAPTER
FOURTEEN

Dawn had only struck Keet as little as twenty minutes prior, and the night's pleasant chill had not yet burned away. Still, the amber bulge on the horizon promised another scorcher. For a planet orbiting such a pocket-size star, Nasako sure got toasty.

The city was oddly quiet, and not just because of the early hour. This was the quiet of absence, of shock and grief. Besides, this was supposed to be a festival that went on for weeks, day and night. There should have been music and fireworks and screams of drunken delight. Instead, all Sheni heard were sobs and the crack and crunch of market stalls collapsing.

He put Alan back down – he'd been squeezing the poor guy so hard, his eyes had almost popped completely out of his head – and together they disappeared into the streets of an older residential district.

Giving the temple's stage a wide berth was the smart choice. Anyone who wasn't a Nasakoan resident was a prime target for mob justice. But the egg was stolen, and the only information the authorities probably had was that a human fled the scene of the crime. The city guards wouldn't just protect an already desecrated temple. They'd be spreading out through the streets of Keet, hunting down anyone who matched his description. They might have even impounded the *Silver Hart* by now.

Xotl. They were waiting patiently in the ship for word of the heist's success. He ducked behind the crumbling wall of a sun-blasted pottery garden, pulled out his data pad, and opened a comm channel with the ship.

"Hello, Sheni," the Xocha spluttered. "How did it go?"

"Not good, man. Thunderskull crashed the party."

"Goodness..." Xotl nervously clacked their beak together. "Is everyone—"

"I'll explain more later," Sheni whispered. "The city's on high alert. Right now our priority is skipping the system, you know? Keep an eye out for anyone trying to clamp the ship. And be ready to leave the second Alan and I get back."

"What about Gecki?" Xotl asked. "Is she—"

Sheni hung up. There wasn't time to play Twenty Questions. The longer their crew spent in the city, the greater the chance they'd be caught and tried for Thunderskull's crimes.

And sure, some of Thunderskull's crimes were their crimes, too. But there was a far cry between sneaking into private property and gunning down civilians. His crew might be thieves, but they always stopped short of becoming proper pirates. They were just in it for the credits. Nobody was ever supposed to get hurt.

Nobody innocent, at any rate.

Sheni ran his fingers through his hair while Alan sat on the ground, smiling at his wrench. Stars above. Everything had gone to... well, it had gone to a great big pile of muloch dung. But he could mope and sulk later. All that mattered now was finding his way back to the *Silver Hart* without getting caught.

"Hop to it, Alan," he said, rising to his feet and checking the coast was clear. "We're not down and out quite yet."

Alan babbled supportively.

They couldn't entirely avoid the market area where the festival had been held. The dock in which Xotl was parked was right on the other side of it. But they could keep to the back streets and crooked alleys wherever possible. Sheni led Alan down a narrow, winding path, listening to the shocked gossip of Nasakoans gathered on the other side of the walls.

He reached a corner, poked his head around it. He swore under his breath. The street was full of locals. Sheni imagined most people had scarpered to their homes when Thunderskull's attack broke out, and were only now braving the outdoors to speculate on what had happened. No way was he strolling past them without somebody alerting the authorities.

He leaned his back against the wall. Directly opposite him was a modest yard of cracked earth. A row of severely dehydrated herbs grew beside a stone bench. Hanging from a wire suspended between the garden's exterior walls was a brown cloak – a more casual version of the outfit he saw the monks in the High Priest's procession wearing. It would be obvious he wasn't a Nasakoan if anyone looked under the hood, but maybe from a distance...

Sheni chewed his bottom lip. He didn't feel great about this. Whomever the clothes belonged to was probably having a bad enough day as it was.

Ah well. He was already wanted for the theft of a priceless krustallos egg. Adding one tatty old robe to the list would hardly make matters worse.

He plucked the robe from the line and pulled it over his

head. His hands stuck out the ends of the sleeves and its hem only came down to his shins, but it was better than nothing.

Alan looked up at him expectantly.

"Sorry, Alan. I don't think anything here fits you."

He searched the tiny yard until he found a wicker basket stuffed under the bench. He sighed. Screw it. In for a penny...

"Hop in and pretend you're a loaf of bread, or something."

Sheni shuffled through the streets, his hooded head down and the wicker basket clutched close to his chest. Whenever he spotted a group of Nasakoans, he crossed to the next street over. Despite a fair bit of backtracking, and a minute or two spent in shadowed alcoves waiting for locals to head back inside their houses so he could pass, he was making decent progress.

It wasn't fast enough, though.

Xotl had tried calling him back. Twice. Sheni set his data pad to silent, just in case. Hopefully the starfish hadn't skipped planet in a panic.

The lid of the basket rose slightly as Alan tried to see where they were going.

"Stop it," Sheni hissed, pushing the lid back down.

He was pretty certain they were headed in the right direction. He'd checked an extranet map while safely out of sight in an old doorway. They were presently climbing a particularly hilly street, which he was pretty sure he remembered descending with Gecki when they first arrived in Keet. Of course, there were a *lot* of hills in the city, and most of the roads looked alike...

Sheni paused to catch his breath. Looking back the way he came, he realised he could see all the way down to where the festival had been held yesterday. A spell of white numbness overcame him. It was a barren battlefield. Most of the stalls were overturned. Stores had been looted and their empty shelves set ablaze. The bodies of guards, pirates and festival-goers alike lay sprawled in the dirt. Chunks were missing from the temple's pillars where they'd been blasted with ballistics and laser rounds.

Unable to remove it from the plinth without Szaladar's medallion, Thunderskull's pirates had smashed the fake egg to pieces. Tiny shards of glass were scattered across the stage, glittering like morning dew on grass.

Survivors were treating the wounded and carrying away the dead on stretchers. Most, however, gravitated towards the stage in various stages of shock and grief. Fake or not, a symbol of their culture – a reminder that there is still hope when the end seems nigh – had been destroyed. Even all the way up on his hill, Sheni could sense the dense, crushing misery that enveloped the local community like a pea soup fog.

He shut his eyes and inhaled deeply.

This wasn't his crew's fault. It was Thunderskull's. If Sheni hadn't stolen Two-Toes's idea, if they'd stayed at the Corpse & Casket and drunk themselves into even greater debt, Thunderskull would still have massacred his way into the Sunrise Temple.

But that hardly absolved him of guilt, did it? If his crew had stolen the egg instead of Thunderskull, the people of Keet would be just as despondent. Breathing, yes, but emotionally savaged all the same. And for what? The sake of a few credits? Keeping a ship that didn't belong to them in the first place?

All this time, Sheni had thought himself one of the good guys. The sort who puts his life on the line when the galaxy needs him. A little rough around the edges, sure, but deep-down ultimately *decent*.

But this wasn't how heroes behaved. And standing on that hill, watching Keet mourn, Sheni came to realise there was a really simple explanation why.

He and Gecki were anything but good.

After three bouts of thumping his fist against the hull, the intercom switched on.

"Hello? Sheni, is that you?"

"Yes, of course it's me. Open the airlock doors!"

The exterior set slid open. Sheni hurried inside with the wicker basket still tucked under his arm. He threw the lid off as the antibacterial jets hissed on from the four corners of the airlock. Alan slowly rose up from the basket like a target in a *Whac-A-Mole* game.

The interior doors opened once the chance of contamination was next to nil. Xotl waited for them on the other side.

"That outfit is certainly... quaint," Xotl said, flexing their arms towards Sheni's scruffy robe. "And we have a new container to go with it. Wonderful."

Sheni pulled off the cloak and dumped it on the metal floor of the corridor, much to Xotl's displeasure.

"The egg's gone. Heist's burned. We've gotta split, you know?"

"And what about Gecki?" Xotl stretched one of their

arms past Sheni to peer into the airlock. "Why isn't she with you?"

"She's gone, too. Thunderskull took her."

"This is very bad." What with Xotl's tone often being so devoid of emotion – strictly from a human perspective, that is – it was hard for Sheni to tell whether they were extremely distraught or calmly admonishing him like a disappointed headmaster. "What's he going to do with her? What are we supposed to do *without* her?"

Sheni marched up the staircase to the cockpit, lost in chaotic thought. Gecki could look after herself, right? Xotl gyrated up the steps behind him in a flopping, rhythmic movement they tended to employ only when either entirely relaxed or under intense stress. Presumably this time it was the latter.

"She told me to get out of there," he explained as he paced back and forth. "She said, 'Make sure Alan and Xotl are okay.' So here I am, you know? Back at the ship, like she said."

"But we cannot leave her behind."

"No, we can't."

"Because she wouldn't abandon any of us."

Sheni stopped pacing the cockpit and raised an incredulous eyebrow in the direction of Xotl's beak.

"You sure about that?"

"Yes. I have absolute certainty. Gecki gave me a job when I needed it, despite the precautions I required, even though she could have just as easily piloted the ship herself. And she went out of her way to save *your* life, if you recall, before you were even part of the crew. She might want everyone to think she's cold and impenetrable, but that's simply a survival mechanism. Underneath those scales, she cares deeply for us all."

Alan stood with his face inches from the rear wall, knocking on it with the head of his wrench.

"Even Alan," Xotl spluttered.

"Yeah, maybe you're right." Sheni shrugged. "Regardless, we've gotta get her back. The ship won't feel right without her smile brightening up the place."

"We know where they were headed." Xotl wriggled down to the pilot's seat. "I marked their camp on the NavMap when Gecki sent me to find Thunderskull's flagship. We can be there in a few minutes."

"Good, man. Good." Sheni sank into his own chair and nodded thoughtfully. "And then we just have to figure out how to free a seven foot lizard from a mutiny of crazy pirates."

"That didn't sound very enthusiastic," Xotl replied, igniting the *Silver Hart's* thrusters.

"Hey, Gecki's the captain, right? Where she goes, the ship follows. And we're taking that freakin' egg back while we're at it."

Xotl twisted their arms around in their seat.

"You still think we can sell the egg? After all this?"

"We won't be stealing it back for us," Sheni said, shaking his head. He jabbed a thumb at the city outside the cockpit windows. "We'll be stealing it back for *them*."

CHAPTER FIFTEEN

The skiff chugged across the city, sporadically dropping in altitude, its thrusters backfiring with coughs and grunts. The harsh, dry wind whipped at Gecki's eyes. She was standing on the exposed deck, surrounded by Thunderskull's raiders. He, of course, was safely below deck with Two-Toes and the krustallos egg. The rest of his goons were grinning through sand-blasted goggles and masks.

She risked a look over the edge of the skiff. Beige huts shot by in a blur. She wouldn't survive the fall. Even so, it might be a better fate than whatever Thunderskull had in store for her.

One of the pirates grew concerned and jabbed Gecki away from the brass railing with the butt of his rifle, just in case. She growled deep in her throat as the bullet hole in her arm flared up, but the pirate only laughed. He needn't have worried. She wasn't going anywhere. Gecki was a fighter, always had been. Whatever waited for her on the other side of this skiff ride, she'd bite its godsdamn head off.

Thirty eight standards. The best part of four decades

she'd been a spacer, taking on whatever jobs she could to survive. Living on the fringe, far outside of Ministerium law. Doing things she wasn't proud of. Working for bosses she'd rather kill. Earning her keep until she could keep what she earned.

She'd been a male back when she first left the nest. The Change came a few standards later, as it did for every Eureptix upon reaching adolescence. Hungrier, she'd been. Less rancorous. Eager to carve a niche for herself in the galaxy. First she'd bought a glorified tug-boat, barely spaceworthy, with a skip drive just powerful enough to jump between systems. Then she upgraded to a two-seater schooner. Finally, through less lawful means, the *Silver Hart*. She even assembled a crew. Never had she reached the heights of spacer status of which that young, male juvenile dreamed, though. No flagships for her. She was just a tired scrounger, drifting through the stars like an asteroid never destined for impact.

But while her scales might be lighter, she'd lost none of her bite.

As the skiff shot beyond the border where Keet met desert, Gecki glanced over her flaky shoulder. Past the shimmering haze of the superheated thrusters stood the enormous rock formation in which the Sunrise Temple had been founded. The first amber tongues of dawn licked up its eastern face.

They'd be fine, wouldn't they? Sheni, Alan, Xotl. They'd escape the city. They could make it out there in the stars on their own.

In *her* ship, she reminded herself with an irritated growl.

Yeah, course they would.

Coz everything came up roses for Sheni.

Minutes later, the skiff arrived at the pirates' base camp. No rappelling this time. A boarding ramp dropped down from the skiff's side. Gecki waited for most of the crew to disembark and then got ushered off the ship with the barrel of a rifle pointed at the small of her back.

The camp matched Xotl's description. Cloth tents, hastily erected by people who didn't care whether they slept under a roof, the stars or a suffocating blanket of booze. Crates of bottles, rifle cartridges and grenades, sometimes chucked in together. A rusty cooking pot suspended over an open fire. She counted twenty-five, maybe as many as thirty pirates and raiders and oddballs in all. Most had been drinking, laughing, not doing very much work while the boss was gone.

The temporary settlement lay right beside the plain's only spot of woodland. The trees were far taller than Gecki expected for a planet so devoid of lush foliage. Some measured more than forty metres. But the forest did circle a lake, she supposed. Thick shrubs and dead leaves formed a dry, brown snowfall around their roots. A flock of angular-looking birds of prey flapped from canopy to canopy, branch to branch, squawking amongst themselves over who might become their next meal.

Gecki hoped it wasn't her.

Above all this, and casting most of it in its elongated shadow, floated the *Howling Rat*. It wasn't a pretty ship. Gecki had seen asteroid crackers with more decorum. Its flanks were patchworks of twisted, superfluous steel. Turrets and cannons had been installed seemingly at random. Not that a pirate like Thunderskull cared how ugly his ship looked. The *Howling Rat* could barge through a battlecruiser and sink half a Queflian fleet. For a psychopathic spacer, that was plenty beautiful.

The rifle jabbed into the base of her spine. Gecki slouched towards the camp. Few of the pirates so much as glanced up at her as she trudged past. Prisoners were a common sight for them, she reckoned. Then again, Thunderskull was pretty cavalier when it came to the lives of his crew. They were probably used to high staff turnover.

They arrived at a cage. It was far too small for Gecki. She guessed they'd brought it just in case the krustallos hatched. Again she was hit with the rifle, this time in the back of her knee, and she crashed to the dirt with a yelp of pain. Gecki twisted around and snarled at the pirate behind her, spittle flying. Even with a gun in his hands, he looked scared enough to piss himself.

"Touch me again and I'll claw your face off," she said, sneering. "Mug like yours, maybe I'd be doing you a favour."

As the pirate took a step back, Gecki quickly assessed the situation. She could make a run for it. It would be messy, but she reckoned she could pull it off. She wasn't handcuffed. Her claws weren't bound with rope. The pirates outnumbered her a few dozen to one, but if she covered enough ground and camouflaged herself before they realised she was missing, it wouldn't matter. They wouldn't have anything to shoot at.

Gecki was still contemplating her escape when somebody snuck up from behind and clamped the collar around her neck.

"What...?" She clawed at the metal choking her throat. "Get this freakin' thing off me!"

She tried to pull it apart, couldn't. She tried to run, but only throttled herself further. The collar was chained to the cage.

"In case you were thinking about going invisible on us," Thunderskull said, smiling pleasantly like a maître d' as he passed by. "You can, of course. But we'll still know where you are."

Gecki rasped and scowled, but said nothing. Thunderskull followed the egg as it was carried through the camp, ready to be transported to the *Howling Rat's* expansive cargo hold. What with Keet on the hunt for thieves, she couldn't imagine the flagship would hang around for long.

With everybody else's attention focused on the shiny treasure, nobody cared about a bashful Two-Toe Tim sneaking over to have a word with her.

"I didn't expect any of this to happen," he whispered. "You and Sheni weren't supposed to be here!"

"You stupid, traitorous scumbag..."

"Traitor? Who went behind whose back, eh? I came to you about this job first, didn't I? I only took it to Thunderskull because you told me you weren't interested!"

"Well, we changed our minds. Happens all the time. Now, get me the hell out of this thing!"

"What, and have Thunderskull cut me out of the take? Kill me, maybe? No way, Gecki. He was the only one willing to give me a place on his ship. I'm sorry it worked out this way, I really am, and I hope Sheni's okay, but..."

Thunderskull clapped Two-Toes on the shoulder.

"Hasn't our boy here done well?" he boasted, grinning as Two-Toes visibly stiffened at his touch. "How much do you reckon that egg'll go for on the market, lizard lady? Thirty thousand credits? Fifty thousand? I've just gotta decide whether I can make more shifting it whole, or by breaking it up into little pieces."

Gecki snorted. Whole. Always whole. Sure, more product sometimes equals greater profit. But small quantities of taaffeite crystal were readily available on the regular market. Whereas a chunk that size? Unheard of. The head honcho of a mega-corp like Negoti or CyberSplice would pay a small fortune to stuff it in their private collection.

Not that she was going to tell Thunderskull that.

"What do you think, man of the hour?" he asked Two-Toes, who swallowed hard.

"I think we should sell it to Peggi Slim, back at the Corpse & Casket," he stuttered. "Let her decide what to do with it."

"Could do, could do." Thunderskull bobbed his keratinous head from side to side. "She takes a cut, which ain't great, but it's quick credits. Fencing takes some of the heat off us, too."

He slapped Two-Toes on the shoulder again, hard enough to make him wince.

"It's certainly an idea."

Gecki realised that the rest of the pirates were already halfway done with breaking down the camp. They certainly looked a lot busier and alert now that Thunderskull had returned from the heist.

"Listen up, everyone," he shouted. They all stopped mid-task. "Today was a success. Shots all round. Even you, Dorphus."

A large gelatinous creature in a chainmail smock grinned uneasily.

"And it's all thanks to our friend Two-Toes over here," he said, pulling Tim over. "So, what d'ya say, fellas? Shall we make him one of our own?"

All the pirates in the camp raised their arms and cheered. Even Two-Toes cracked a nervous smile.

"I dunno, fellas." Thunderskull shrugged. "It sounds like you don't like him…"

Everyone cheered even louder. Whistles were added. Gecki took the opportunity to tug desperately at her chain again.

"All right, all right. Well, I guess if you *really* want him to tag along with us, you know what to do..."

The three pirates closest to Two-Toes rushed forward and grabbed him by the arms. At first Two-Toes kept smiling, dismissing it as just some harmless part of the initiation ceremony. But then they kicked out his knees and bent him over one of the packing crates. He tried to break free, but any one of the pirates could have probably pinned him down alone.

"Come on, guys. What is this? I got you the egg, didn't I? Don't you have a pledge, or something? Tell me what you want me to say!"

"Don't make me change my mind, Timothy." Thunderskull strolled over to the cooking pot. "Every new arrival goes through this. It's tradition. Ain't that right?"

Everybody grunted in the affirmative.

"See? Now, do you want to join my crew or not?"

Thunderskull had been holding some sort of metal rod in the fire. Now he pulled it out, and Gecki saw it was a branding iron – the same branding iron that had been used on his first mate, Qorgin, by the looks of it. The head glowed a sinister yellow-white.

The pirates pulled down the collar of Two-Toes's shirt. His wriggling became even more erratic, his boots carving shallow furrows in the dirt, but his body remained exactly where they wanted it.

"You know what? Forget the job. Just give me a cut of the credits and I'll disappear."

Thunderskull raised the iron.

"And where would you go, Two-Toes? Now everyone will know you belong to me."

He slammed the branding iron down on the back of Tim's neck. The human screamed, a high-pitched, blood-curdling wail that made Gecki's teeth itch. Her nostrils flared at the stench of burning flesh. A few of the pirates around the camp laughed, but most of them looked as unsettled as Gecki.

Thunderskull pulled the iron free a few seconds later. Strings of melted skin dripped onto Tim's shirt. Somebody chucked a bucket of cold water over his neck. Gecki thought Tim might have passed out from the pain, but he shivered and whimpered as steam rose from the bloody mark.

Thunderskull snapped his fingers together, then waggled one towards Gecki.

"I know just where to send you," he said with a psychotic grin. "The Dogg Pitt's always in need of new fighters. Violent gal like you's gonna love it."

CHAPTER SIXTEEN

As Xotl took off over Keet, Sheni sat forward in his seat and cradled his head in his hands.

This was all his fault.

Gecki was right – he always assumed things would work out fine in the end. And in fairness, they usually did... for him. He should have died many times over, yet here he was, still breathing, still being a thorn in the galaxy's backside.

When Earth fell, he hadn't been fortunate enough to secure a ticket for one of the Arks destined to shepherd the remnants of mankind to a new world amongst the stars. Most people hadn't. So just prior to lift-off, he snuck aboard through a temporary sewage pipe that hadn't been fully detached yet.

He shivered at the memory. Not his finest moment. Certainly not his cleanest.

Could it have killed him? Probably. He hadn't known for sure there'd be a valve to open the waste treatment tank from the inside. Nor that the force of lift-off wouldn't kill him, what with him having no restraints or pills to manage the g-force. But he was a risk-taker. (Another word for a gambler, he realised with a sinking heart.) It was a much better plan than staying behind on an irradiated Earth and waiting to die.

And it paid off, didn't it?

Of course, it had only taken a few days for security to find him. He supposed it had been inevitable – he hadn't exactly put much thought into what came next, and the ration bars and water bottles in his backpack were only gonna last so long. Getting to humanity's new homeworld was all that mattered, not how comfortable he was during the journey. And once he was onboard, they couldn't exactly kick him off, could they?

Oh, but they could.

They'd kept him in a holding cell for a while, which had been all right. He slept on a mattress instead of a galley grate, got three meals a day, climate-controlled air *and* a toilet. But he couldn't stay on the ship forever, apparently. There 'wasn't room'. They 'didn't have the resources'. Sheni knew that was a load of crap. He'd heard about the Platinum Sector. The richest of Earth's elite had paid for guaranteed passage. While regular Joes put up with coffin bunks and protein paste, the nought-point-one percent got luxury suites and Michelin star restaurants. There was plenty of food to go around... just not for the likes of him.

And yeah, he was a stowaway. That hadn't helped.

So when the authorities next scheduled a trade with the Ministerium, they stuffed him in the shuttle's hold along with half a dozen supply crates and took him to some barren rock with a name like a barcode. And they left him there. It had a breathable atmosphere, so it wasn't totally barbaric of them, but his chances of survival were still next to nil. Worse odds than if he stayed on Earth, ironically. And when raiders ambushed the Ministry traders, because of *course* they did, he'd quickly gone from prisoner to captive.

Not exactly his greatest run of luck.

He should have died there, too. Either those marauders would have eaten him, or he would have slowly starved to death. His new companions weren't exactly the hospitable sort. Sheni had never seen an alien before – humanity was still a good few years from joining the wider galactic community – and even those rabid humanoid freaks scared the bejeezus out of him.

And then Gecki showed up. She'd been tracking the raiders for a while, waiting for them to set up camp somewhere so she could steal what they'd pilfered. Tied to a wooden stake in their dank cave, Sheni had watched as a shimmering shape scuttled across the moist walls. It paused by the litany of treasures, accidentally knocked over a golden lamp, then snaked its eerie way towards his post. He'd pulled his legs in sharply as the creature forewent her camouflage. Of course, Gecki was the most terrifying thing Sheni had seen in his life. A towering reptile with plaque-covered teeth, one eye that was psychotic and yellow and another that was milky and blind, and a snarl that turned his bowels to water. Much worse than the raiders. But instead of tearing a chunk out of him, she'd cut his ropes, pointed to the loot she wanted him to carry, and let him follow her back to her ship.

That was the first time he met Xotl and Alan, too. He couldn't understand a word either of them said, and his natural response had been to curl up like a foetus in the corner of the cargo hold. He'd cried. He'd soiled himself – not that he'd ever admit that to anyone, especially Gecki. And all he did was shut his eyes and whimper when Gecki stalked over to him and injected a translator chip into the back of his neck. Funny how the universe became mildly less intimidating once you knew what everyone was trying to say.

"Coming up on the camp now," Xotl spluttered, yanking Sheni out of Memory Lane. "No sign of the *Howling Rat*. Stars, the camp looks quiet, too..."

Sheni clasped his hands in front of his face, then stood up. He owed Gecki his life. That wasn't in question. He'd been a strange, alien creature tied to a post in a cave, and she'd taken a chance on him. They couldn't exchange so much as a single word, and *she'd taken a chance on him*. And sure, she never let him forget it. Gecki was always going on about how she wished she'd left him to rot on that stake, or begging him to leave her and find a ship of his own. But that was just Gecki being Gecki. He could see what Xotl meant now. Meanness was her way of being affectionate.

And what did he do to repay that debt? He lost their credits on holo-races. He sent his crew on dangerous missions without weighing up the risks. He got his rescuer kidnapped by a bunch of deranged pirates for the sake of a stupid egg.

Yeah, Gecki was right. He made everyone else shoulder the consequences of his mistakes so he could live carefree.

Well, not anymore.

"Don't worry, Xotl." He fist-bumped one of the bemused starfish's arms as they landed the ship. "We're getting Gecki back, whatever it takes."

The ramp dropped down, the airlock hissed open.

Sheni tiptoed out.

The camp was deserted. In some ways, this was a good thing. True to his impulsive nature, Sheni hadn't really considered what he would do if he found the camp full of pirates. Get shot or stabbed, most likely.

Of course, in a much more practical sense, this was about as far from good as Sheni could get. They'd raced here in the *Silver Hart* to rescue Gecki. A severe lack of cantankerous lizards sure made his job difficult.

"We're too late," he said to Xotl, holding up his data pad. "They're already gone."

He let his arm fall to his side and spun in a circle, hoping to spot somebody on the horizon. There was nothing around for miles, just rocks and cracked dirt.

"Dammit!" he yelled at the empty plains. A few birds took flight from the nearby trees.

"I'm scanning the skies," Xotl replied. Sheni peered up at the ship; he could see Xotl's purple arms flicking switches on the cockpit's dashboard. "Look around. See if they left anything useful behind."

Sheni stepped carefully into what remained of the camp site. What did the starfish expect to find in there, a map? A pirate itinerary? He doubted half of Thunderskull's crew could even read. It looked like a bunch of teenagers had got drunk in the woods. Broken bottles, pieces of a shattered chair, a tangle of wires someone had missed. A lot of churned mud. Everything stank of urine, mammalian body odour, and something else Sheni couldn't quite put his finger on. Charred meat, perhaps.

"Argh! There's nothing here, Xotl. Just a bunch of empty cans and spent bullet casings." He kicked over an old wooden bucket. "They could be anywhere in the galaxy by now, you know? We're screwed."

"Not necessarily. Check the fire."

"What?"

"Check the fire, Sheni."

It took him an embarrassingly long time to find it. He was looking for a flame – you know, a *fire* – but what Xotl meant was the pathetic mound of black stones half-hidden beneath a plastic crate lid. Tiny curls of light grey smoke gasped from its base. He reached out, drew his fingers back, and then tentatively gave the stones a prod.

"The coals are still warm," he said, tossing a lump into the air. "They can't have left too long ago, right? We can still catch them up!"

"Not the *Howling Rat*, unfortunately. I'm not seeing anything of that size on the scans. It's left Nasako's outer orbit at the very least. And as you say, Thunderskull could have skip-jumped to practically any system by now."

"You spineless twerp, Xotl." Sheni was tempted to pick up another lump of coal and throw it at the cockpit's windows. "Why'd you let me get my hopes up like that?"

"Because there is another, much smaller ship. An unregistered transport schooner about eight thousand kilometres above our present location. They appear to be preparing their skip drive."

"So? There are ships everywhere, Xotl. Space is full of them!"

"Do you think a place like Keet gets much traffic? Isn't it worth a shot, Sheni?"

He exhaled and bit down on his lip. There were billions of planets in the galaxy, and Gecki could be headed for any one of them. Might as well ask him to find a brain cell inside Alan's head. Wild goose chase. Never gonna happen.

Whatever it takes.

"Course it's worth a shot," he said, jogging back to the airlock. "If she's not there, we'll ask around at the Corpse & Casket. If nobody at the bar knows where she is, we'll check out Thunderskull's old haunts. We'll search every star if we have to, and we won't stop until we find her."

CHAPTER SEVENTEEN

How in the stars was this thing supposed to skip them halfway across the galaxy when it had barely survived breaching the atmosphere?

Gecki cast a critical eye over the shuttle. She was no engineer, but prior to discovering Alan pottering about inside the *Silver Hart's* engine room, she'd always had to maintain her own starships. She knew when a vessel was on the verge of popping a few bolts.

It would have surprised her if this one had any bolts left to pop. Surely it was held together with nothing but rust and bad intentions. She supposed that given the life expectancy of a pirate or raider was usually measured in months, not years, there wasn't time to worry about such trivial stuff as health and safety.

They left worrying about that sort of thing to their prisoners instead.

It was a small shuttle, which, if she were trying to remain optimistic, left fewer things to go wrong. It only had two primary compartments. The hold, in which she presently resided, and the two-seater cockpit up front. Both seats were occupied by a pair of Thunderskull's pirates. The door connecting the two cabins remained wide open. Another precautionary oversight. If the cargo hold suffered a sudden depressurisation event, the pirates would be killed in seconds.

Not that her frozen corpse would mind the company.

The hold carried a strong, metallic smell, and she doubted that was due to the hull alone. Dark patches stained the dull aluminium. She thought she saw globules of meat rotting in the cracks between panels beneath her feet. Other prisoners had been brought through here. Tortured here. *Died* here. And nobody cared enough about the victims, the ship, or even themselves to consider hosing away the leftovers. Grim stuff.

Two rows of chipped, plastic seats lined the port and starboard walls. The airlock – the only way in or out, as far as she could tell – occupied the rear wall, directly opposite the door leading to the cockpit. A lone light bulb hung in a cage on the ceiling beside loose wires and loops of chains. A mag-locked crate in the far corner to Gecki was fastened to the floor with leather restraints.

She was almost afraid to yank the chain connecting her metal collar to the grate on the wall in case she ripped part of the hull off, but she tried anyway. All she achieved was an abrasive *clang* noise, an uncomfortable vibration through her seat, and another pang of pain in her wounded arm. Not surprising. These restraints were designed to keep an Alpha Rhoden captive. Not that she'd give up, of course. But realistically speaking, she wasn't going to break herself free.

"Hey, hey," one of the pirates yelled back at her. "Settle down back there. We're tryin' to think."

"Comes more easily to some of us than others," the second pirate added, chuckling to herself.

Pirate One punched Pirate Two in the arm. Gecki rolled her eyes. Yeah, she was gonna die out here. They were drunk. And not just drunk from when they'd been toasting a successful heist back in the camp. Even now, a bottle of Oortilian whiskey was being passed back and forth between the two of them. She wondered if Thunderskull would laugh if he found out, or cut off both their heads.

"You can let me out at the next somnium station," she said with a sneer. "I'm happy to walk the rest of the way."

The pirates stopped trying to figure out the ship's faster-than-light controls and turned around in their seats. Gecki knew she was no looker, even among other Eureptix – she'd been prettier as a male, if you asked her, before she lost the eye – but godsdamn, these idiots were ugly. Like the people in those Ficasso paintings Sheni had tried showing her once.

One of them – Pirate Two – clapped her companion on the shoulder and climbed down from the cockpit.

"You ain't getting off nowhere," she said, revealing a mouth missing half its teeth. "Not till we get to the Pitt."

Pirate Two was a feather-templed Kerulian who wore more straps and belts over her pink torso than actual items of clothing. Not that Gecki was one to judge. She recoiled as a tangible cloud of booze assaulted her slitted nostrils. At least it did something to hide the body odour. All mammals stank a little, but this one? *Eesh*. Take a mud bath, sister.

She desperately wanted to lash out and slit the Kerulian's throat, but Thunderskull had made the sensible call of tying her hands before she was put on the shuttle. She was strong, but not strong enough to pull through these knots. Gecki made do with a snarl instead.

"Oh, man," Pirate Two continued. "The Dogg Pitt. Been years since I last put on a bet there. You ever seen it?"

"No."

"Ah, well, you will now! Glorious, it is. Big jewel of a gladiator arena. Never goes three minutes without a fight. Sometimes tourneys, sometimes winner-stays-on. Churn through fighters quicker than I get through ale, they do." She squinted at Gecki. "I fancy your chances, actually. Might stick around after we sell ya, put some credits on your match. Depends who they face you against, though." She scowled, ruminating on a past match. "Not all the competitors fight fair."

"Pity," Gecki growled. "I know how important following the rules is to scum like you."

"Run that mouth all you want, Lizard Lady. Just remember who's gonna be on which side of the cage, yeah?"

Gecki had heard rumours of the Dogg Pitt before, just had zero interest in checking the place out for herself. The space station travelled from system to system to evade the Ministerium. The peacekeepers tended to turn a blind eye to places like the Corpse & Casket, but the Pitt dealt in slavery and mass murder. Hunters kidnapped potential victims from every corner of the galaxy, from Scrap Rats to stone trolls. The deadlier the fighter, the more the Pitt paid for them. But whether they lasted one match or one hundred, nobody got out alive. Well, not unless they became a slave master themselves.

"All righty," Pirate One said, raising the bottle of whiskey in triumph. "Skippin' to the Acamar system in three... two... one..."

Nothing happened. The view outside the cockpit windows remained the same – a bunch of stars, and a hell of a lot of vortex nebula (or as Gecki had decided to call it, the Big Purple Bruise). She felt the floor shudder as the skip drive beneath their feet failed to start properly.

"What's happenin'?" Pirate Two stomped her way back across the hold. "Why ain't we goin' nowhere?"

"You shorted out the drive core," Gecki sighed. "We'll probably go supernova any second."

"Shut up, reptile!"

"Nah, that ain't it," Pirate One said, blearily checking the dashboard's diagnosis. "Says here we…" He raised a fist to his mouth to suppress a hiccup. "Says here we've got a proximity alert. Can't jump while we're next to anything with mass."

"Then you must'a broken it, you dummy! We're in space. There ain't nothing next to us, not for miles!"

A second, much more violent crunch shook the ship. Pirate Two stumbled backward and only kept herself from falling on her rear by grabbing one of the chains dangling from the ceiling.

"Yeah, drive's dead." Gecki reached up, her wrists bound together, and scratched the scales underneath her chin. "I'd sail this ship back to solid ground, if I were you."

Pirate Two pulled a six-inch blade from the sheath slung over her chest and brandished it at Gecki.

"I swear, you overgrown skink, if you don't stop talking—"

"Maybe set her down somewhere unpopulated, though…"

"—I'll cut off each and every one of your scales and rub salt into your flesh. Cook you over a freakin' spit."

"Sounds delicious. And Thunderskull will be *so* happy when you come back without any payment from the Pitt." Gecki grinned. "Yeah, he won't space either of you for sure."

"Won't both of you shut your damn traps?" Pirate One screamed down from the cockpit. He'd sure sobered up fast. "I think we're being boarded!"

Gecki listened as Pirate Two slowly backed away from the airlock doors. There *was* a faint hissing sound, the sort that accompanied two docks linking together. Huh. She guessed she'd been wrong about the skip drive. Well, that's why every good ship needs an Alan.

"Unfortunate for you, isn't it?" She grimaced toothily. "Sort of ironic, in a way, you getting hijacked by raiders. Not much difference for me, though. Your ship, their ship – it's all the same."

"They'll kill you, too!" Pirate One shouted as he tried – and failed – to disengage the shuttle.

"Yeah, maybe," she rasped. "But die now, or at the Pitt? Least this way's quicker."

Everybody fell silent as the airlock performed its standard preparatory cycle. Pirate Two pointed her knife at the doors. Pirate One stared at them, the shuttle's flight controls forgotten. Gecki, privately far more concerned than she would let either of her captors know, used this moment to try and wriggle out of the ropes binding her wrists.

"What the hell are they doing?" Pirate Two whispered nervously when the doors failed to open. "What's taking them so long?"

Gecki glanced up from her ropes. The airlock process *was* taking an unusually long time. Pirates did have a flair for the dramatic, she supposed. Or maybe they didn't plan on actually using the airlock – maybe they were just tethering the ships, ready to cut their way through the hull and space everyone inside.

Then, without fanfare or warning, the doors slid open. A murky wave of gas billowed out. Gecki took a deep breath. Gods knew what chemicals were being pumped into the shuttle. Knock-out gas for one species caused fatal paralysis in another. Before the mist became too thick to make out much more than dark shapes, she saw Pirate Two cover her mouth with her arm, for all the good that would do.

Gecki rubbed her wrists together, ignoring the increasingly painful burning sensation, and pulled sharply on the chain keeping her collar linked to the hull. She was not dying in here. Not tied up like some rabid zoo specimen.

A figure suddenly sprinted into the shuttle from the airlock. Bipedal, humanoid, mildly muscular. Gecki couldn't make out much more than that. It raced towards Pirate Two wielding some kind of club. Pirate Two raised her knife at the last second, but it was too late. The assailant swung the club into the side of her head. The crunch was audible. Pirate Two hit the floor like a fleshy anvil. Gecki suspected she wasn't getting back up again.

Pirate One snapped out of his stupor. He reached across the cockpit and snatched up what looked, from where Gecki was sitting, to be a rifle. But by the time he'd sat back up and aimed it towards the cargo hold – a stupid decision, given they were in a shoddy shuttle in godsdamn space, but the sort of braindead idea Gecki expected from those in her line of work – the mystery figure had already climbed up to the cockpit and driven their club halfway through his skull. The rifle clattered down the pair of steps into the hold.

Gecki resumed her desperate rope-rubbing. The dark shape in the fog bent down slightly as if catching their breath, then slowly stalked towards her. She growled deep in her throat, hoping to scare it off, knowing that whoever it was could easily kill her where she sat...

"All right, Xotl, that's enough," the figure said, wafting their hand through the gas. "Stars above, it's like a Krolak marsh-party in here."

"Sheni?" Gecki rasped.

"Who else did you think would rescue you?" Sheni

emerged from the mist with a smirk on his face and Alan's bloodied wrench in his hand. "We're the only friends you've got."

"How in the galaxy did you do all this?" she asked, as the gas began to clear.

"Xotl reconfigured their decontamination chamber to pump out warm water vapour into a cold airlock. Figured it was the only way to get on board without being shot."

"Very clever. Now get this collar off me!"

"Oh, yeah. Give me a second..."

Sheni rummaged through the dead pirates' pockets. The more the mist dissipated, the more frequently he turned his head and clasped a hand over his mouth. There was more brain on the floor than Gecki expected.

"Oh, God..." Sheni groaned, "this was much easier when I couldn't see them..."

"They were gonna sell me to slavers at a fighting pit, if that helps. They had it coming."

"I mean, yeah, that does ease my conscience... Ah, bingo."

He hurried back with a rusty, old fashioned key in his hand. Gecki bared her teeth as Sheni fumbled with the lock on the collar. Then it snapped apart, and she launched herself out of the chair, tearing viciously at her ropes with her teeth.

Sheni, meanwhile, crossed to the supply crate in the opposite corner.

"What are you doing?" she snarled, her words muffled by the rope in her mouth.

"Checking for loot, what else?"

He unfastened the straps and flung open the lid. Nothing but a bunch of raider rags lay inside.

"Ah, damn. I was kind of hoping the egg would be here too, you know?"

Gecki finally chewed through the rope, spat it onto the floor and flexed her sore wrists.

"It hasn't grown smaller since you last saw it, you cretin. Obviously Thunderskull still has the egg with him."

"All right, genius. Stars above. You're welcome for the rescue, by the way."

Gecki shrugged. "I was gonna escape anyway," she snarled.

Sheni set his jaw, slowly shook his head, and then, much to Gecki's surprise, caught her in a hug.

"It's good to have you back," he said with a wink, his head pressed against her chest.

She flinched in disgust, softened reluctantly, and then finally wrapped her scaly arms around her crew mate. A couple of pats on the back was okay, she supposed. It wasn't like anyone was watching.

"As if I was going anywhere," she rasped.

CHAPTER EIGHTEEN

The shower on the Silver Hart was pretty decent, as one would expect on a luxury starship, though years of neglect had left its cubicle a little scummy. It offered two distinct modes: water and air. Not every species enjoyed getting wet, and for some of the hardier, more leathery citizens of the galaxy, a fierce blast of abrasive oxygen was far more effective at scrubbing off the day's dirt.

Sheni, being a normal man who preferred his skin not to feel as if it had been attacked with a cheese grater, always chose the former option. Gecki opted for a combo; first the air to clear the muck from between her scales, and then a generous (sometimes *too* generous, when others were waiting their turn) torrent of hot water to remind her of the rock pools back on her home planet. Xotl, despite their starfish appearance, didn't really care for water, and rarely needed a shower anyway given they never left the ship. And nobody knew what Alan did to keep clean. Quite frankly, nobody *wanted* to know.

Sheni wandered down the corridor to the cockpit, wearing a fresh set of clothes and rubbing a towel over his head. Gecki, Xotl and Alan waited for him inside. Gecki had a bandage over her arm where she'd been shot and a packet of painkilling meds on the desk beside her. She stabbed him with an impatient glare.

"What?" he said, taken aback. "I'm a mammal. I sweat. That planet was, like, a hundred degrees. And no way was I doing anything until I'd scrubbed the blood from under my fingernails."

He retrieved Alan's wrench from his back pocket.

"Oh, and, erm, I gave this a wash, too. Thanks, dude."

Alan bounded over with a big smile on his face, took back his favourite wrench, and gurgled gratefully.

"Time is running out, human." Gecki pointed a claw towards the cockpit windows. "And Thunderskull is getting away."

He stopped towel-drying his hair and squinted at Xotl.

"You told me he'd *already* got away, didn't you?"

"He's still in the system," Gecki snapped. "Or he was, before you decided to pamper yourself for half an hour."

Sheni rolled his eyes, dropped into his chair and tossed his towel over the side of the nearest terminal. Xotl visibly shivered.

"Let us be rational," the starfish said, clacking their beak nervously. "We rescued Gecki. In anyone's book, that's a huge win. It's a shame we couldn't get the krustallos egg back too, but there will always be more credits. We all left Nasako with our lives. There's no need to throw them away going after Thunderskull, is there?"

"More credits?" Gecki scoffed. "Not if Slugbarrow takes our ship, there won't be. May I remind you all that we only have a standard rotation left to pay back what we owe?"

"Perhaps we could sell the shuttle?" Xotl was referring to the cruddy pirate skiff to which the *Silver Hart* was still tethered. "It's a poor quality model, but its components should cover our debt."

"That's true." Gecki tapped her claw against her snout. "Be easier to fence, too, given it's unregistered. Could even sell it direct to someone in need of a ship at the Corpse & Casket. Have to space the bodies and mop up the blood first, though."

Now it was Sheni's turn to shiver.

"And who wants to fly it back to Barataria?" he asked. "Xotl has to stay on this ship, and Alan can't, so I guess it'll be you, Gecki."

"You'd be coming with me," she growled.

"And my company will make you feel safer with a dodgy skip drive beneath your feet, will it? Come off it. Besides, no pirate with a spare three and a half thousand credits is gonna buy that heap of junk. Especially not if they find out we stole it from Thunderskull."

"This is true," Xotl mused disappointedly. "If Thunderskull found out, the buyer wouldn't just be out of pocket. They'd be out of blood and breath and everything else they require to stay alive, too. It wouldn't be worth the risk, either to them or us."

"Which is why we need to steal that egg back," Gecki said, baring her teeth. "Think how many credits we'd get for something like that. Enough to pay off our debts and live comfortably for another cycle." She growled deeply. "We can't keep scraping by. We're better than that."

"Which is exactly why we should steal it back, yes." Sheni reclined with his fingers laced together behind his head. "And also why we need to return it to the people of Keet afterwards."

"Give it back to the Sunrise Temple? Are you mad?" Gecki took an angry step towards him. "Wait. Are they offering some kind of reward? Because that could be smart, you know... get us the credits *and* make us out to be the heroes..."

"Nope, no reward. Not that I know of, at any rate. But it's the right thing to do."

"The right thing to...?" Gecki stalked the rest of the way across the cockpit and laid a patient claw on Sheni's shoulder. "I can see the heat has got to you. It's made you forget that we're thieves. Pirates, spacers, all-round scoundrels. We steal things, remember? Nothing about what we do is" – she shuddered – "*right*."

"Exactly! And like you said, *we're better than that*. We answered the call to defend Kapamentis. For years we tried to only steal from those who don't deserve what they've got. But I messed up, and then we got desperate, and here we are stealing a holy artefact from a city of good people who need it far more than we do. Sure, we're thieves. But I don't think *this* is what any of us want to be. Right?"

Gecki growled in frustration and stomped back to her own chair, her short tail flicking back and forth in irritation. Xotl's arms wilted. Alan waved his wrench around like it was a toy aeroplane.

"I'd rather be rich and keep my ship than give that egg back to a bunch of tentacle-faced flag-wavers who don't appreciate its market value," Gecki grumbled, "but until that egg's in our possession again, none of that matters. And the longer we spend yapping about the moral implications of our profession, *Sheni*, the less chance we have of getting it!"

"Yeah, about that. You said Thunderskull's still in this star system. What the hell's he doing, hanging about like there isn't a whole planet after him?"

"Charging his ship. That's what I overheard him say to

his crew before they hauled me into that shuttle, anyway. A ship like the *Howling Rat* takes a lot of fuel to run, and it's not like Thunderskull's welcome in most ports. Those giant thrusters on its belly and stern? Electrostatic ion engines."

"Okay...?" Sheni shrugged. "So, what? Is he plugged into an interstellar charging station, or something? Where's he getting that kind of juice?"

"I don't know Thunderskull well, thank the stars, but I know that he won't spend a credit on something he can just take for free. And there's somewhere in this system where a guy can collect a lot of energy very freakin' quickly, if they're the sort willing to take a risk."

"A *very* big risk," Xotl added darkly. "The Sydney-Wilson Vortex might be slow, but it eats planets. Any ship caught in that..."

Sheni stood up and approached the windows while Gecki and Xotl debated the survivability-proximity ratio of the vortex nebula. The Purple Sunset, as the Nasakoans referred to it. A starless smudge against the cosmic backdrop, best visible whenever lightning bolts the length of moons crackled through its billowing amaranth folds.

Creeping death.

"So Thunderskull is somewhere in that thing?" he said, turning back to his crew mates.

"Somewhere *next* to that thing," Gecki said, correcting him. "Even in that armoured flagship of his, going inside the vortex spells annihilation."

"And what happens when the ship's batteries are recharged?" Sheni had no idea how electrostatic ion engines worked, and he didn't care who knew it. "He'll skip out of the system? Where?"

"No idea. Didn't overhear much else. Too preoccupied with being dragged along by my collar." Gecki growled at the memory. "My guess is he can already skip system. Skip drives need somnium to work, and he ain't getting any of that from the nebula. He's just filling up his regular tanks while doing so's free."

"So once he's gone, he's gone." Sheni nodded in thought. "This is our one shot at getting that egg back before he disappears for good."

"As the pilot of this ship, I feel it is my duty to remind you both that the *Silver Hart* is a luxury starship, not a dreadnought." Xotl cartwheeled onto a different pair of arms. "It is not equipped to withstand that kind of pressure. The Sydney-Wilson Vortex tears whole worlds apart. The slightest miscalculation and we will be first dismantled, then quickly crushed into our atomic components."

"You'd better not miscalculate, then," Sheni replied with a friendly wink.

Xotl uttered a spluttering, clacking curse that Sheni's translation chip failed to decipher.

"Hold onto your mammary glands," Gecki said to Sheni. She'd never cared to fully grasp human biology. "We might be running out of time before Thunderskull skips town, but there's no way we're rushing into this without a proper plan. We know where your brainless attitude gets us. Mountains of debt, framed for thefts we don't even profit from, and shipped off to fighting pits with leashes round our necks. Swinging our way onto the *Howling Rat* is gonna get us killed."

"As is going anywhere near that vortex," Xotl added sternly.

"Hectopascals," Alan giggled, popping up from behind a computer terminal like a demented gopher.

"I hardly think Thunderskull would let us fly anywhere near his flagship, anyway," Sheni said. "Not unless it was to satisfy his own curiosity. Those cannons would blow us to pieces. We shouldn't bring the *Silver Hart* within a hundred klicks of that place."

"Thank the stars," Xotl said, their arms relaxing.

"I thought you wanted to return that big lump of taaffeite crystal to the good people of Keet," Gecki replied sarcastically. "And now it sounds dangerous, you're just giving up?"

"Giving up? Nah. Just thinking things through, you know? The only way we're getting that egg is by boarding the *Howling Rat* without Thunderskull realising. So that's what we've gotta do."

"Oh, is that all? Sounds easy." Gecki tipped her head back and hissed. "Gods, Sheni. Do you have a teleporter, or something? Coz otherwise, how the hell are we s'posed to do that?"

Sheni crossed to the other side of the cockpit and pointed to the third-rate shuttle still connected to the *Silver Hart* by their conjoined airlocks.

"We've got everything we need right here."

Gecki followed Sheni's eye line. When she turned back to him, she did so sporting a mischievous, sharp-toothed grin.

"Now *that*, Sheni, is a half decent plan."

CHAPTER NINETEEN

Sheni and Gecki studied each other.

"I mean..." Sheni tilted his head. "We don't *not* look like Thunderskull's raiders, right?"

"You more than me," Gecki rasped. She didn't look entirely comfortable with the concept of shirts and trousers, let alone all the belts and straps she'd pilfered from Pirate Two's corpse. "These leg tubes don't even reach my ankles. But his crew is made up of all sorts. With these duds, I'm sure we'll blend right in."

Sheni threaded his arms through the sleeves of the jacket he found in the supply crate.

"Thunderskull did boast that there were always more suckers willing to join up, remember? Anyone asks, we're just the new arrivals. Fresh from the Dogg Pitt."

Gecki grinned.

"Yeah, that's good. I like that."

They added as many trinkets and trophies to their outfits as they could find. Sheni noticed that Gecki was having a little trouble moving her shoulder.

"How's the arm?"

"Ah, it's fine," she grumbled. "Bit stiff, that's all. Bullet went right through. It'll heal quickly enough. If not, I'll just tear the whole arm off and grow a new one."

Sheni paused and scrunched up his nose.

"That... shouldn't be an option."

"I'm kidding, you stupid human." She snorted in amusement. "Eureptix doctors only consider regenerative amputation a last resort."

Sheni's eye fell on the half-naked bodies of the two dead pirates propped up beside one another on the port-side row of seats. He exhaled through pursed lips.

"I know they had it coming and all, but I do wish we could leave them looking a little more dignified, you know?"

"We can space them on the way to the *Howling Rat*. Can't risk bringing them on board with us, anyway."

"I don't think drifting through space forever is much of an improvement."

"And I don't think they care. They're dead."

"I mean, you're not wrong..."

Sheni bent down and picked up the backpack they'd use to carry the egg. It was heavier than he expected.

He undid the flap.

"Alan. We told you already, you're not coming with us."

The top of the green menace's head poked out. He fit inside the backpack the way corned beef fits a can. His red-handled wrench slowly rose beside him like a periscope.

"It's going to be dangerous," Sheni continued. "The people we're visiting aren't very friendly."

Alan hooked his wrench through the clasp of the flap and slowly pulled it back down over his head. Sheni sighed and swung the backpack over his shoulder.

"Looks like we're a team of three," he told Gecki.

"Urgh, whatever." Gecki stomped up to the shuttle's

cockpit, the buckles and zips on her clothes jingling as she took her seat. "We don't have time to trick him into staying with Xotl. If he runs off and gets lost, he'll be Thunderskull's problem."

Sheni smiled. He knew Gecki would secretly be devastated if Alan chose to maintain any ship but hers.

"I'll keep an eye on him. And I'm sure he'll help us keep an eye on the egg."

"Which one?" she snarled, watching Alan peer out at her through a gap in the fabric.

"Which egg?"

"Which *eye*."

"Are you both ready?" Xotl asked over the shuttle's comms. "Disconnecting airlocks now."

Sheni gripped the seat in front of him hard as the *Silver Hart* disengaged from the shuttle with a perilous shudder. Both sets of airlock doors had already been fully shut and sealed, but he never liked being reminded that only a few inches of plastic and metal separated him from suffocating in the void. Especially when he wasn't even on his own ship.

"We're clear," Gecki said to Xotl. "Still in one piece, for now."

"This hunk of junk will get us to the *Howling Rat*, right?" Sheni whispered. "Like, for all the jokes, nothing's *actually* gonna fall apart?"

"Only one way to find out. Hold on for your life..."

Gecki triggered the shuttle's thrusters and shot away from the *Silver Hart*, which Xotl had fortunately already repositioned out of harm's way. The walls of the shuttle trembled; the chains dangling from the ceiling swung backwards and became tangled with an almighty crash. Sheni gritted his teeth and shut his eyes, expecting a breach at any second. Alan gurgled gleefully from his backpack.

"Readouts all seem normal," Gecki rasped, reading the diagnostics on the shuttle's retro dashboard. "Engines are painfully in need of a service, but operational. You can let go of that seat now. Actually, sit in it. It's time to ditch our friends."

Sheni plonked himself down in the passenger seat beside Gecki, the backpack clutched in his lap. Gecki pressed a button to seal the cockpit door shut, then a second series of buttons to open the airlock doors at the rear of the ship. The shuttle shook from the change of pressure – another agonised grimace from Sheni – which was followed by a series of leaden thumps.

"And there goes our cargo," Gecki said with a wicked smile. "Sorry, guys. Guess you won't be betting on those fights after all."

Sheni felt a morbid desire to watch their bodies drift away. He'd heard that corpses in space actually boiled long before they froze. Something to do with there being no convection in a vacuum. But the shuttle had no rear-view camera feed. He just had to take Gecki's word for it.

"Do you still copy, Xotl?"

"I hear you," Xotl replied. "I'm performing a long-range scan of the section of vortex closest to Nasako. It shouldn't be too hard to detect a ship of the *Howling Rat's* size. Head towards the coordinates I've sent to Sheni's data pad. You'll probably see it before I do."

"How long will it take to get there?" Sheni asked, showing Gecki the coordinates.

"With a skip drive, seconds," she replied. "But there's no way I'm risking using that piece of crap. Half an hour with the basic engines, I reckon."

Sheni sagged further into his seat and fiddled anxiously with the straps of his bag.

"Let's hope Thunderskull doesn't fill his tank before we get there..."

Something that sounded vitally important went *clunk* above their heads.

"*If* we get there," Gecki rasped ominously.

The next twenty minutes dragged, but none of the shuttle's fuses blew, nor did the wires spark and ignite or the cockpit window crack and induce explosive depressurisation. They chugged through space like a rusty old tugboat, barely a word passed between them, the big purple bruise in the sky growing greater and greater still.

Xotl had sent over more precise coordinates about halfway through their journey, and lo and behold, the *Howling Rat* was exactly where the starfish said it would be. Lurking on the very edge of the nebula, its skiffs stashed in its hangars, its open decks locked down. Two sheets of hexagonal cells had unfurled from the rear of the ship. Every few seconds, a colossal bolt of lightning would scream out of the purple cumulonimbus and strike one of them, dissipating in ripples of static, charging the enormous batteries that generated the *Rat's* thrust.

"Only a pirate like Thunderskull would be stupid enough to go near that," Sheni said quietly.

"Thunderskull, and us," Gecki reminded him.

The shuttle's comm unit crackled as it switched to a receiving channel, surprising them both.

"Ungula, Skort," said a scratchy, weaselly voice. "What the stars're you doing back so soon?"

Gecki looked pointedly at Sheni. With a minute shake of his head, Sheni gestured towards the comms. Gecki rolled back her eyes, exasperated.

"It's the *Howling Rat*," she rasped. "Reply to them."

"Me? Why *me?*"

"Well *I* can't speak to them, can I? They're expecting to hear the pilots, not their prisoner! But humans, Kerulians, whatever..." Gecki shrugged dismissively. "There ain't *that* much difference."

"That's speciesist," Sheni hissed. "I won't sound anything like them!"

"More than I will! I don't even have a diaphragm!"

Sheni set his jaw, shook his head, and then reached across to the comm controls.

"Yeah, 'bout that," he replied, trying his best to sound tough. "Lizard broke free. Nearly tore..." He paused. Was he pretending to be Ungula or Skort? "Nearly tore Ungula's head off. Had to space the bitch."

Gecki fixed Sheni with an open-mouthed glare hot enough to melt tantalum. He winced and shrugged apologetically. They waited to see if the radio operator would question Sheni's voice.

"Stars, man," the operator replied. "That's cold. Captain's gonna be pissed."

Sheni and Gecki both deflated with relief.

"Erm, yeah... don't tell him about this, okay? I'll set things right with the big guy myself."

"Hey, it's your funeral. Unlocking the hangar bay doors for ya, but be quick about it, all right? Lightning gets in here, we're all toast."

Gecki waited for the comm line to cut, then punched Sheni on the arm.

"See? You humanoids all sound exactly the same."

"Helmets," Sheni said suddenly, rummaging in the container next to his seat. "We'd better put them on before anyone gets a good look through these windows."

They squeezed into a pair of metal raider helmets covered in spikes and dents. Sheni's smelled of cigarettes and grease. Gecki's was too snug against her snout and muffled everything she said, but it fit. Sheni's jaw was visible; Gecki's face was hidden entirely. If it weren't for the exposed claws on her hands and feet, she might have passed for someone without scales.

"Gently does it," she said, guiding the shuttle on a haphazard path toward the open docking bay. "Gods, I can hardly see out this stupid thing..."

A lightning bolt zigzagged dangerously close to the shuttle and splashed over one of the outstretched charging cells. The lights in their ship hummed slightly brighter for a short moment.

"Oh, I don't like this at all," Sheni moaned.

"It's *your* plan. A smart one, too, for once."

"Yeah, and the smarter a plan, the more opportunities for it to go wrong..."

The hangar was relatively compact, with only enough space for three ships. As their shuttle passed through a flickering forcefield, Sheni recognised the skiff to their right from back in the Sunrise Temple, when it had hovered above the krustallos's cavern and cast down the ropes for Thunderskull's escape. Parked beside it was a two-seater speeder. The bay to the left was empty, presumably reserved for the shuttle. Gecki clumsily navigated it into position and shut off the engine.

They looked at each other – or at each other's raider masks, at least – in anxious trepidation.

"I guess we're doing this, then," Sheni whispered, as he watched one of Thunderskull's goons march along the catwalk suspended over the hangar.

"Don't forget to bring the guns," Gecki rasped, standing up and unlocking the door to the cargo hold.

"It's just the one gun, actually."

"What do you mean, just the one gun?" Gecki stopped on the steps and watched Sheni check the rifle's magazine. "And why do *you* get it?"

"Because *you've* got claws. Besides, it's just window dressing, you know? It's not like I'm going to use it."

"You'd better not," she growled. "This needs to be a quick one. We grab the egg and scarper. Nobody can know we were here. We're keeping that gun, though."

"Oh, absolutely. You can have first dibs to play with it when we're done."

There was no trace of the two dead pirates in the cargo hold, except for a red smear next to the airlock door where one of them must have hit their head prior to being sucked out. Sheni shivered. Gecki said the shuttle had been in desperate need of a wash before he rescued her, so chances were nobody would notice anything amiss if they did decide to inspect the vehicle.

The airlock opened. Metal steps clattered halfway down to ground level, then got stuck. Gecki gave them a kick and they unfolded the rest of the way. Sheni took a deep breath and followed her into the hangar, whose industrial doors were already rumbling shut over the forcefield.

"Keep it cool," Gecki rasped quietly as they crossed the hangar floor. "Act like we're supposed to be here and chances are no-one will question us."

"I don't suppose you've got any idea where Thunderskull's cargo hold is?"

"Not a clue." She hissed in frustration as she tried to scratch the scales on her snout but couldn't. "We don't even know for sure that's where he's keeping the egg. Might have it in his private quarters. But this ain't some Plillup or Queflian ship. Its hold will be in one of the usual spots. We'll figure it out."

"Ship this size, that could be a dozen different places. And how are we gonna get inside?"

"Look at you," she rasped. "You stop long enough to come up with one half-decent plan and now you're afraid to improvise."

"I'm not afraid to improvise, Gecki. I'm afraid of having my skin flayed. Big difference."

The security door opened automatically upon their approach. Fortunately, the *Howling Rat* didn't require keycards to pass from one section of ship to another. A consequence of high staff turnover. In fact, outside of the hangar, most of the different compartments didn't even have doors. They'd just be a hindrance, what with most members of the crew constantly rushing about from deck to deck.

Sheni stepped to one side as a four-armed Luethian jogged the other way down the corridor. His heart pounded. Beads of sweat rolled down the inside of his helmet. But the pirate didn't so much as glance at him on his way to the hangar. Gecki was right. If they acted like they belonged there, everyone would assume they did.

So, no more flinching. No more stepping aside. From here on out he was Sheni Dupont, bloodthirsty raider for hire. And he didn't make space for *no-one*.

His impatient companion shoved him forward.

No-one except Gecki, of course.

The ship's corridors were as barebones as Sheni expected. Exposed pipes, wires bunched together like messy French braids, panels missing from the walls. He'd been on a few big pirate and raider ships in his time, most often without their owners' permission, and they were all alike. Minimal upkeep, minimal cost. You wore something out until it broke, then you either fixed it up with whatever materials you had to hand, or you threw it out and stole a replacement. These weren't the grand, gold-trimmed galleons of Old Earth's buccaneers. These were spacer pirates, their ships flying fortresses. And while the outsides could withstand a nuke, the innards were often one bad swabbie away from falling apart.

Gecki seemed to follow the ship's paths at random, turning sharp left at times, descending staircases, seemingly looping back on herself. They passed a messy bunkhouse full of hammocks and nests and crusty-cushioned cubicles, a mostly empty mess hall full of wooden benches that wouldn't have looked out of place somewhere in the Corpse & Casket space station, even a laundry room – presumably only for Thunderskull's sake, because the rest of the crew certainly didn't use it. For a while, Sheni kept pace without comment. They needed to keep moving, to keep giving everyone else the impression they were headed somewhere important. And it seemed helpful, at first, to get their bearings. But eventually he had to say something. He could feel Alan growing restless in his backpack.

"We're never going to find the cargo hold like this," he whispered, pulling Gecki into a nook. "We could have walked by it already and not even realised."

"What do *you* suggest, then?" she snarled in return. "You want to stop and ask someone for directions?"

"Maybe! New recruits must have trouble finding their way around, you know?"

"No, Sheni, I don't know. That sounds like a good way to get ourselves caught."

"Well, we have to do *something* soon." He waited for a pair of pirates to stroll past. "We don't have forever to search this place. Thunderskull will skip the *Howling Rat* out of the Morg system as soon as his ion tanks are full, and then we really will be screwed."

"Helical fasteners," said Sheni's backpack.

"I know," Gecki said, snapping her claws together. "The engines. There's always a map of the ship down in the engine rooms. Only way to know where all the pipes go."

"And the engines are always at the back of the ship," Sheni replied, pointing an enthusiastic thumb behind them. "Engines, map, treasure. See? I love a plan, me."

They hurried down more corridors towards the stern, taking stairs down to the lower decks whenever the opportunity presented itself. A small room housing one of the flagship's numerous rotary cannons was on their left, and Sheni overheard an insectoid gunner yell something about needing a second crate of reserve shells. It sounded as if the crew was getting ready to leave.

Sheni could tell they were close to the engine room even before he heard the roar of machinery or felt the temperature rise by a few degrees. The hairs on his arms and the back of his neck stood on end. He could practically taste the static in the air – a sharp, metallic and strangely salty sensation that made his tongue feel fuzzy. Raiders in welding goggles and greasy overalls twisted valves and pumped levers. Steam hissed from poorly fitted pipes. Toward the back of the primary hall, two huge, cylindrical batteries stood like silver grain silos. Branches of ghostly blue filament discharge crackled between the Tesla coils at their peaks.

Alan raised the flap of the backpack slightly and cooed.

"Where do you think we'll find the map?" Sheni asked. He found himself having to speak at a normal volume again to be heard.

"No idea. Do I look like an engineer to you?" Gecki growled impatiently. "Probably wherever they keep their tools."

Sheni looked around for a workshop, a notice board, a storage unit of any kind. Somewhere central and easy for the crew to locate, something that might house a list of schematics, physical or otherwise. But the whole sector was, much like the rest of the ship, a form of organised chaos. Only those whose lives were spent forever within its walls could hope to understand whatever systems – if any – the mechanics had in place.

He turned onto a narrow gangway running between the electrostatic tanks and almost barrelled into a scruffy, unarmed pirate coming the other direction. They were struggling to carry a large chrome canister. Sheni tilted his head down and avoided making eye contact.

"Excuse me," he said in the gruffest voice he could muster. "Comin' through."

But the pirate didn't step aside. Instead, he slowly bent down to look under the face-guard of Sheni's helmet. Sheni's heart fell as he recognised the glum face staring back at him.

"Sheni?" Two-Toe Tim asked. "Is that you?"

CHAPTER TWENTY

Gecki slammed Two-Toe Tim into the wall of the canister storage shed, a secluded alcove in the engine room Sheni hoped no-one else could see, especially since Gecki had taken the opportunity to remove her helmet.

"Cry out, I dare you," she snarled, curling a claw before his eyes. "I'll slice you from throat to navel."

"She's not kidding," Sheni added, frantically checking for witnesses.

"Why the hell would I sound the alarm?" Tim wheezed. He tried to smile at Gecki, but it came off like a grimace. "I don't want you to get caught. I want you to take me with you."

"Did you hear that, Sheni?" She laughed. "He wants to come with us. We said no the last time you wanted to join our crew, and you ended up stealing our haul and shooting me in the arm. Why in the stars would we take you now?"

"That was Thunderskull," Tim pleaded. Gecki was pushing him so hard against the wall, the plywood was bending out of its frame. "I had no idea you guys were going after the egg too. And I don't want to join your crew, honest. I just want passage off this ship. You can drop me off wherever you like, I swear."

Gecki and Sheni shared a dubious glance.

"I thought all you wanted was to find yourself a crew," said Sheni.

"Yeah, I did too. But look what the bastard did to me!"

Gecki already knew what Tim intended to show them, and she relinquished her grip on the man's chest. He peeled back the collar of his bloodstained shirt. Some of Tim's skin peeled back with it.

Sheni recoiled not just from the sight, but also the sudden odour of burned flesh. Thunderskull had branded Tim with his insignia, and not particularly cleanly at that. The wound was covered in blood, pus and blisters.

Alan popped up from the backpack and gave Two-Toes a sniff.

"Bacon," he gurgled.

"I knew Thunderskull was bad news even before you warned me to keep my distance," Tim continued, wincing as he pulled his shirt back into position. "But I thought I'd be part of something bigger. Like, a member of a family, or something. I'd pull my weight. Earn my keep. But nah. I'm just another part of his collection, tagged and chucked on board with the rest of the loot."

Tim twitched as a sharp pang of pain ran across his shoulders.

"You think this brand is something I can get surgically removed, yeah? Like, reconstructive surgery? Not that I've got the credits for an op like that…"

"This isn't a rescue mission, Two-Toes." Sheni shrugged. "You made your bed. Sneak off next time you're at shore, so to speak."

"What do you mean, it's not a rescue mission?" Tim nodded to Gecki. "You came here to rescue *her*, didn't you?"

"*She's* my captain. That's different. And no, I broke her free hours ago."

"And you came back here anyway?" They all flinched as Tim's incredulous voice momentarily rose louder than the surrounding machinery. Remembering himself, he followed with a hushed whisper. "God, how stupid are you?"

"We want that egg," Gecki snarled. "It's rightfully ours."

"It's rightfully the Nasakoans'," Sheni reminded her.

"You still care about that stupid thing?" Two-Toes shook his sweaty head in disbelief. "Well it's not down in the engine room, you idiots. It's safely stashed in the vault on the second deck."

"Second deck," Gecki rasped to Sheni. "That's a start. Let's go."

"You know you'll never get in there, right?" Tim started after them as they turned to leave. "Thunderskull keeps it locked up. Doesn't trust his crew any more than he does anyone else."

"We'll figure something out," Sheni replied with a wink. "We always do."

"Not without the access code, you won't. The hold's security door is as thick as the hull. You ain't getting in, not before the *Rat* sets sail for another system."

"And let me guess," Gecki said, her upper lip curling back. "You know how to bypass the security."

"Better than that." Tim smiled with a mix of enthusiasm and desperation. "I know the code. His crew brought me on board at the same time as the egg, and I watched him unlock the vault. He didn't think I saw, but I did. Pretty sure I remember it correctly. Promise to take me with you when you leave, and I'll get that door open for you."

"Tell us the code now," Gecki rasped. "Just in case."

"No way." Tim crossed his arms. "If Thunderskull catches me helping you, I'm dead. Either you bring me with you, or you can leave here empty handed."

"You won't get a share of the take," Gecki insisted.

"There won't *be* a take," Sheni said through gritted teeth. "We're not selling the damn egg."

"I don't care about the credits," Tim said, letting his arms fall to his sides. "I just want to be anywhere but here."

"We've wasted enough time already," Sheni whispered to Gecki. "It'll be a lot quicker if he helps us. We can drop him off at Kapamentis or the Corpse & Casket when we're done. And I mean, look at the guy. He's one chipped nail away from taking a stroll out the airlock."

Gecki studied the despondent human and growled.

"Fine," she snapped. "At least this way I can make sure you don't run off and tell Thunderskull we're on board."

"Oh, I won't be doing that, I can assure you." Two-Toes laughed sadly. "I know how good work is rewarded around here…"

Gecki put her helmet back on and reluctantly allowed Two-Toes to lead the way. Sheni felt sorry for the guy, really. Sure, the guy was a cretin for signing on with Thunderskull's crew. He had to be a few loaves short of a bread basket, choosing to become a pirate to begin with. Sheni was different. He'd been exiled. He didn't have a choice. But while Tim might be an idiot, he didn't deserve to be scarred and branded and put to work like a mad scientist's Igor. Plus, he was human. These days, they were almost as rare as a krustallos.

Speaking of which…

"We need to talk about what we're doing with that egg,"

he whispered to Gecki as they followed Tim out of the engine room.

"No we don't," she rasped back. "We're taking it to Peggi and getting the credits we need to pay off Slugbarrow. Whatever's left will go on repairs and stuffing our pantry. I'm the captain of the *Silver Hart*. My word is final, got it?"

"You sound like Thunderskull," he said, knowing it would get under her scales. "An authoritarian dictator who only cares about the bottom line."

"Oh, give me a break. I only care about the ship and my crew, which includes you, in case you've forgotten. Without those credits, I have neither. Don't you dare compare me to Thunderskull. I'm doing what's best for all of us."

"All right, fine. I didn't mean it. But we can't keep the egg, Gecki, and we can't sell it. Seriously. You didn't see how devastated the people of Keet were. This isn't just some lump of taaffeite crystal, you know? It's not some expensive paperweight going to waste. It's a symbol of hope for the future. Without it, they're just an ignored community waiting for their planet to die."

"And that's our problem, is it?"

"If we keep that egg for ourselves, then yes, it is."

Gecki growled and grumbled to herself. Sheni didn't think he had her convinced. The cantankerous reptile had spent decades fighting dirty to get by. She wasn't likely to let morals get in the way of her survival now.

Down the same corridor they travelled before, up a flight of rickety steps. At the top they encountered a pair of armoured raiders. Sheni watched as Two-Toes squeezed past them, half-expecting the guy to rat them out the first chance he got, or for the raiders to question what Two-Toes was doing with two strangers who didn't belong on the ship, but they barely even acknowledged Two-Toes was there. He was of little more importance to them than the rats scurrying about in the brig.

"Not far now," Tim whispered. "Just a few halls down on our left..."

And there it was – an enormous round vault door locked in place by a wealth of pistons and bolts and clamps. An archaic computer terminal jutted out from the wall beside it. Two-Toes was right. There was absolutely no way he and Gecki were getting inside without the access code, not without shutting down the entire ship's power or deploying a tactical nuke. The damn thing didn't even have a handle to pull.

"Okay," said Tim, nervously licking his lips. "Now all we have to do is—"

Three raiders – one crocodile-like Krolak and two Oortilians with jagged scars running down their blue faces – stormed out from a narrow gangway to their left. Sheni's muscles tensed up; Gecki flexed her claws. The Krolak performed a double-take as they spotted Two-Toe Tim.

"Ah, there you are!" one of the Oortilians barked. "What're you doing all the way up here? You heard Thunderskull. Those coolant canisters ain't gonna empty themselves."

"Yes, of course." Two-Toes gave Sheni a flustered look as he spluttered out his reply. "I was just... I just needed to—"

"Engine room, now! Before the batteries blow!"

Two-Toes took a step toward them, then leaned back toward Gecki and whispered the access code in her earhole. Gecki snarled and nodded. Tim then followed the three pirates back down the stairs toward the thrusters. One of them smacked him around the head for a laugh.

He glanced back at them with eyes that begged, *Save me.*

And then he was gone.

"Eh, we got the code." Gecki turned to the computer. "He got revenge on Thunderskull, in a way."

"You know we still have to get him, right?" Sheni checked both ways down the corridor. The coast was clear. "We had a deal."

"Deals change. And he didn't *technically* get us to the egg. Not all the way."

"Gods, Gecki. Remember how pissed you were when Thunderskull stole the egg after we'd already claimed it? Are you really gonna break your promise? Break the *code?*"

Gecki inputted the last in a ten-character sequence of runes and waited for the vault door to unlock. She roared in frustration.

"It doesn't matter. The stupid human's password doesn't work!"

Sheni leaned over her shoulder and pointed at the screen.

"Swap this rune out for that one," he said. "They look similar. Two-Toes might have got confused, right? *I* can't tell the difference."

She tried the new combination. The moment she typed out the final rune, clamps released, bolts shot back into their iron sleeves, and the vault's circular door groaned open.

Even with a mask of dented metal covering her face, Sheni could tell Gecki was grinning.

"First we get the egg," she rasped, rolling her eyes behind her helmet. "Then we get your human friend. *Maybe.* If we don't get shot trying."

"There's the lizard I know and love," Sheni replied, smiling as he gestured for Gecki to head inside. "Your blood might be cold, but deep down you've got a warm heart."

CHAPTER
TWENTY-ONE

Gold glittered in Gecki's eyes.

"Now that," Sheni said, beaming as he pulled off his helmet, "is a lot of loot."

He'd never seen so much treasure in his life. Piled up high against the vault's bland, industrial walls were baskets of ancient gold coins, silver goblets and bronze statuettes, priceless paintings still in their ornate frames, antique furniture from half a dozen different empires, idols of gods long forgotten, dusty bottles of centuries-old wine. None of it sorted, labelled or categorised. Just tossed in like trash.

Alan hopped out of Sheni's backpack with his wrench in one hand and an old hessian sack clutched in the other. He scarpered across the mountains of doubloons in gibbering ecstasy.

Gecki pulled the vault door as close to shut as she dared, not wishing to accidentally lock themselves inside until the next time Thunderskull had some treasure to dump. Or to switch off the lights, for that matter, which presumably ceased to operate once the bolts and clamps re-engaged.

She was salivating like a greedy dragon by the time she turned back to the golden hoard.

"This collection would keep us minted for a lifetime," she rasped hungrily. "Screw the egg. This is where the real credits lie."

"How are you going to move it all?" Sheni scoffed. "You got a truck I don't know about? For the first time in years, you've got pockets. Fill 'em."

While Gecki hunted for the most valuable artefacts she could feasibly carry, Sheni searched for the krustallos egg. Hopefully Two-Toes hadn't been mistaken when he said Thunderskull stashed it there. He slipped trying to scale a small mound of purple gemstones. Stars above. Why didn't Thunderskull sell some of this crap? He could retire and live out his years on a tropical beach somewhere. But Sheni supposed it was less about the credits for him, and more about the power he wielded over everyone else. The lunatic actually *enjoyed* being a pirate.

Gecki, unable to put up with her constrictive helmet any longer, tore it off and chucked it into one of the piles. Sheni doubted anyone would notice it didn't belong there. Perhaps in years to come it would be passed on as a priceless relic, sold to some gullible collector under the pretence it once belonged to a pre-Ministerium warlord.

"Oh, that does *not* taste good," she said, after taking a swig of some of the dusty wine. She sneered and pointed a claw at the bottle. "That's how you know it's worth a lot."

"Daylight robbery," Alan tittered, filling his sack with random trinkets.

Trust a treasure vault to make Gecki forget about the countdown to the *Howling Rat's* departure. Sheni shook his head and left the two of them to it while he continued his search for the egg. It had to be around here somewhere, he assured himself as a river of marble-like orbs cascaded over his boots. Pirates were notoriously lazy, so they wouldn't have carried it far. Not unless Thunderskull insisted. And it wasn't as if it could roll off on its own...

"I found it!" He waved his hands above his head. "Both of you, get over here!"

It was even more beautiful when surrounded by glittering gold than nestled away in a dank, gloomy cave. Every craggy inch of its surface glistened with a serene, blue shimmer. Sheni was afraid to even reach out to it, the light made the crystal appear so sharp. And when he did lay his fingers upon the shell, it wasn't cold to the touch as he expected but exuded a deep, reassuring warmth.

He swung his empty backpack onto the ground and tried to lift the egg into it. He couldn't. Gecki snickered with laughter, then bent down to help him. But she froze the second her claws brushed the egg.

"Erm, what?" Sheni stared at her expectantly. "You gonna pick it up or not?"

"Trust me, I know my way around an egg," she snarled. "And this one's about to hatch."

Sheni had been crouched beside it. Now he scurried away on his backside. Hatch? Yeah, he'd known the egg belonged to the krustallos. He'd even seen its calcified corpse back in the temple. But it was just an artefact, right? He hadn't seriously considered the possibility that something living was curled up inside it, biding its time to break out...

"It can't hatch here," he babbled. "This isn't supposed to happen until the egg's back in Keet!"

"That krustallos will hatch wherever it godsdamn pleases," Gecki rasped. "But if you think you can explain

Nasakoan tradition and municipal boundaries to the baby, be my guest!"

Alan bounded over with his sack of goodies slung over his shoulder and cooed at the egg excitedly. Sheni thought he saw it wobble slightly and hoped it was just the surrounding riches shifting from everyone's footsteps. But then it shook again with increased vigour, and that was when Sheni knew Gecki was onto something.

"So much for selling the taaffeite in one big chunk," she grumbled.

"We can't have a krustallos flying about." Sheni shook her by the shoulder. "The pirates here would probably kill it. And how are we supposed to get it back to the temple? Tie a piece of string around its leg and pull it around like a kite?"

"Once the krustallos hatches, it won't need its egg anymore." Gecki shrugged and scratched her scales. "Neither will the Nasakoans. The shards will still go for a pretty high price..."

"Stop thinking about credits and *do* something!"

"It's an *egg*, Sheni. What do you want me to do, un-incubate it?"

Sheni's heart climbed into his mouth as a hairline crack suddenly snaked down from the top of the egg, followed by another a few inches to its left. A third bridged the two as the taaffeite crystal wriggled and bulged...

A triangular fragment cracked free. It slowly rose from the rest of the egg...

A tiny wyvern head leered bashfully from underneath and stuck out a pink, forked tongue.

"N'aww," Gecki rasped. "Look at the little hatchling."

Alan giggled as the baby krustallos licked his eye.

Sheni bit his fingernails. Could he bring a live krustallos

back to Keet instead? Of course he could. There was no question as to whether High Priest Szaladar would accept it, right? It was supposed to be their civilisation's guardian. But all those Nasakoans at the festival... the entire celebration had been building up to watching the egg hatch...

"Wait, I've got an idea." He rummaged around in the side compartments of his backpack. "I'm sure I still have some in here, you know, for patching up spacesuits and stuff..."

He triumphantly held up a roll of duct tape.

"Oh, wow." Gecki crossed her arms. "You're really doing this."

"We just have to keep that krustallos inside the egg until it's back at the temple." Sheni unravelled a stretch of tape. "It's been growing in there for two or three weeks, right? A few more hours won't hurt."

The krustallos was still wearing the shard of shell as a hat. Sheni gently pushed it back into place.

"Back you go," he whispered. "Nighty night."

"Hard boiled," Alan gurgled.

Sheni quickly taped over the cracks, then added a few more strips across the egg for good measure. There. Good as new. So long as they looked at it from a distance no closer than thirty metres, no-one would tell the difference.

"Help me get it in the bag," he said to a bemused Gecki.

"I don't know what's come over you," she replied, scooping up the egg, "but you're acting godsdamn weird."

"I'm just trying to put things right," he sighed, pulling open the backpack. "The galaxy's much bigger than the *Silver Hart*, Gecki. It's certainly bigger than our debt to a slime bag like Slugbarrow."

Gecki mulled this over as she slotted the egg inside. Sheni clasped the backpack shut. It was a snug fit, but hopefully that would keep the little critter from bursting out of its shell again. He could still hear it chirping inside.

"Right." He heaved the straps over his shoulders. It was damn heavy, but he could handle it. "So we just need to figure out how to rescue Two-Toes on our way back to the shuttle..."

A klaxon ran out throughout the ship. The lights in the vault switched from a pale yellow to a bloody red. Alan covered the spots where his ears should have been. The pistons around the enormous circular security door hissed as it prepared to lock them inside.

"Is that alarm for us?" Sheni asked, grimacing.

"No, Sheni, it's for the other stowaways," Gecki replied sarcastically. She shoved him toward the vault door. "Screw Two-Toes. We need to get off this flagship *now*."

CHAPTER TWENTY-TWO

Gecki pushed against the vault door as Sheni and Alan hopped through the slowly diminishing gap, then slithered out just before it could slam shut. They immediately ducked as a pair of bullets flew past their heads. Well, Gecki and Sheni did. Alan stood where he was, smiling blissfully, a good few feet short of the crossfire.

"Which way back to the shuttle?" Sheni shouted, flinching backwards.

"That way," Gecki snarled, glancing to their right. "Or maybe... no, definitely..."

Sheni brought up the rifle he'd stolen from the raiders and began firing back at the pirates rushing down the hallway to their left.

"How about we care less about which way is right," he yelled, "and more about which way we can go *right now?*"

"Through here," Gecki replied, pulling him and Alan around the corner.

They sprinted down a narrow passageway of exposed pipes, fuse boxes and gas tanks. Sheni looked back over his shoulder and saw a shadow block the light at the entrance, so he fired a couple of shots back the way they came. Somebody cried out in pain, so he guessed at least one of the rounds found its target.

He would have felt bad, but, you know. Pirates.

"Was the shuttle on the second or third floor?" he hissed at Gecki.

"Why do I always have to remember everything?"

"Because you're harder to kill, so I have more to worry about!"

Gecki growled before grudgingly adding, "Third floor."

They reached the end of the passageway where it met the corridor running parallel down the other side of the ship. Another glance behind told Sheni that nobody was following them through such a narrow gap. They must have seen what happened to the first person who tried and decided it wasn't smart to pile into a bottleneck. He raised his rifle again, just in case.

One of Thunderskull's raiders jumped out at them from the corridor ahead with a grin on his face and a knife in his hand. Sheni couldn't turn his gun around fast enough in the cramped passageway. It didn't matter. Gecki connected a fist with the raider's nose. It cracked, as did the skull behind it. The goon collapsed to the floor, briefly choked on his own blood, and then fell still.

"I see a stairwell," Gecki said so casually, it was almost like she hadn't just killed someone. "If you keep an eye on the path behind us, I reckon we..." She snarled irritably. "Where's Alan?"

Sheni spun around. A pair of gangly green legs were poking out from a steel duct a few metres back. Sheni rushed down to grab him.

"Alan, don't go in there!"

He was too late. Alan's legs slipped out of reach just as

Sheni got to the vent. A pair of gormless eyes stared back at him from the dusty gloom inside.

"Stop being an idiot, Alan! We don't have time for this!"

"No, this is good," Gecki rasped, peering into the duct. "You're heading to the shuttle, aren't you, Alan? Get the engine warmed up for us, all right?"

Alan babbled agreeably, banged the top of the vent with his wrench, and then waddled off into the darkness.

Sheni groaned and ran his hands down his face. The lunatic would get himself killed. When he turned back to Gecki, she was ripping away the rags and belts of her disguise.

"Turn around, you freak!"

"Seriously? *Now* you believe in modesty? It's not like you normally wear any clothes."

"It still feels weird when you watch me take them off!"

Sheni anxiously faced the other way down the passageway until Gecki was done. The shrieks and whoops of pirates hungry for a fight grew steadily louder. Gecki stretched her arms, flexed her tail and shifted the colour of her scales to match the copper-brown corridor.

"Much better," she snarled. "Now check your ammo and summon every last ounce of irksome Sheni luck you've got. We're gonna make a run for it."

Alan was not headed back to the shuttle.

People assumed that Alan was stupid, but in truth he just had a very particular way of thinking. That's how he'd kept the *Silver Hart* from catastrophic system failure on twelve different occasions, despite the rest of the crew's best attempts to push the ship beyond its modest limits. And though his bulbous eyes might struggle to focus on the same thing at the same time, they were more than capable of spotting all the cannons and turrets and interstellar missiles lining the *Howling Rat's* flank.

If they took off in the shuttle while Thunderskull and his minions were on the hunt for them, they'd be reduced to space-dust long before they reached the *Silver Hart*. And then, because he didn't exactly seem like the sort of guy to practice restraint, Thunderskull would likely blow the *Silver Hart* up, too.

Simple he may be, but, as with the ship's engine room, Alan liked all his component pieces to stay in the right place.

The metal panels of the ventilation shaft buckled and popped back into shape behind him. His bag of loot jostled and jangled on his back. It was too dark to see anything, but that didn't bother Alan. On a ship like the *Howling Rat*, the scariest things lurked in the light. And besides, he knew exactly where he was going. He'd already been there once before.

The duct sloped downwards to the floor below. Alan slid down the chute and giggled. There was no use in doing anything if you weren't having fun.

After a couple of minutes, Alan arrived at the vent's end. It was noticeably hotter here than back in the passageway. His head slowly rose from the opening like a green sun creeping over a horizon.

Yes, he was in the engine room.

Alan hopped out and waddled across the hall. Only one of the busy engineers glanced up at him, but, after a second of surprise and bafflement, she decided everything was fine and went back to work. Alan looked like the sort of critter who belonged places. Like rats and safety inspectors. Plus, he was smiling. Nobody who smiled like that could possibly be a threat to anyone.

The emerald orb scurried around the back of the giant battery tanks being charged by the nebulous lightning storm outside. He could squeeze into spots others couldn't, which came in handy when repairing things. Came in handy when breaking things, too. He found a particularly important-looking set of pipes linking the two tanks and used his wrench to loosen their couplings. A jet of steam hissed out of one. A crackle of static leaked out from the other.

Alan dribbled at a job well done.

"Calamitous thermionic expulsion," he gurgled to himself.

The clock was ticking. Time to go find his friends.

"Remember, I'm only shooting at you because you're shooting at me!"

Sheni didn't especially enjoy firing guns. Certainly not at people, regardless of their species. He preferred to adopt a quieter, laid back attitude, one which didn't include being perforated with bullets or having body parts melted by lasbeams. But as Sheni liked to remind himself, he was a survivor. If it was a choice between him and the people trying to cut him out of existence, well...

Besides, he didn't need to actually *hit* anyone. He just needed to keep them busy.

Taking cover behind a monitoring device boasting a dozen pressure dials – half of them with needles in the red – Sheni watched as Gecki dropped down from the ceiling above the three pirates shooting at him. They were too busy firing their guns to notice the slight warpage in colour behind them. She lashed out with her claws, carving gashes through their throats, arms and bellies. The first two were dead (or seriously wishing they were) before the third even realised he was the only one still shooting at anything. Gecki flicked the blood off her hands as Sheni jogged down the hallway to join her.

"There'll be more," she snarled.

"Shuttle's that way, right?" Sheni said, pointing back the way they came.

"Yeah, but so are the pirates." Gecki nodded to the nearby stairs. "I say we head up to the top deck and loop back on ourselves. By the time these idiots catch on to what we're doing, we'll be halfway across the system."

"Not with a busted skip drive we won't."

Gecki sneered and punched Sheni on the arm. It hurt.

"Stop worrying about everything, human. It all works out fine in the end, right?"

"Yeah," Sheni said with a sigh, "I can see why you found me so irritating..."

He ducked as a bullet pinged off the bulkhead beside him. Gecki was right. They couldn't shoot and stab their way through an entire crew of bloodthirsty pirates, so up and over it would have to be. He raced for the stairs. The shimmering outline of Gecki's camouflaged form already stood waiting for him at the top.

"Oh, I'm not sure this was any better," he said, as he realised where they were.

The bow of the *Howling Rat's* upper deck was encased with interlocking panels of see-through aluminium, a material as transparent as glass but four times as strong. Completely impractical, in Sheni's opinion. He'd take strength and security over a fancy view any day. Fortunately for Thunderskull, the *Howling Rat* had shields to deflect projectiles, asteroids and wayward bits of debris. And Sheni had to concede it *was* an impressive view. You couldn't truly appreciate the majesty of a star system-devouring vortex until you'd witnessed its deadly stellar clouds up close.

Underneath the transparent dome, on a raised wooden platform in desperate need of an old-timey ship's wheel, stood Thunderskull. He was barking furious orders at a handful of lackeys whose bowed heads clearly indicated they wished they were anywhere else in the galaxy. The rest of the helm was occupied by heavy shipping containers and the cranes needed to move them.

Also on the upper deck were about a dozen heavily armed pirates, who immediately and mercilessly opened fire on the two intruders.

"How's the egg?" Gecki shouted after they both dove for cover.

"Intact, mostly," Sheni replied from behind the crate opposite hers. "But I can feel the krustallos wriggling about. I don't think it likes the shooting any more than we do. We need to get it back to Keet, pronto!"

"Worry about getting off this ship first. If we can do that, reaching Keet will be easy!"

"So now you're happy to give the egg back to the Nasakoans, huh?"

"Ha! We just don't need it anymore, that's all. Why do you think I was so keen for Alan to head back to the shuttle? He's the one with the bag of riches!"

"Sure. It's not that you've grown a conscience, or anything."

Gecki grinned and rubbed the tips of her claws together. Her smile fell as a grate inches from Sheni's feet lifted up and an excitable Alan hopped out.

"What in the stars are you doing here?" she snarled. "We told you to get on the shuttle!"

Alan lowered his wayward eyes and dribbled.

"What did you do, Alan?" Sheni's blood ran cold. "Alan... What did you do...?"

A heavy tremor rumbled through the ship's hull. The big brass pipe beside them blew a gasket. Sheni shut his eyes.

"Please tell me you didn't set the engines to explode. We've talked about this, Alan. If you *have* to blow something up, wait until we're not on it first!"

"Shut up, you idiots," Gecki said, nodding past their hiding spots. "Haven't either of you noticed we aren't being shot at anymore?"

Sheni anxiously poked his head past the corner of his crate. All of the pirates had backed off. Thunderskull remained on his elevated platform, but now he was facing them instead of his lackeys. Sheni would have suggested this as the perfect time to sneak off back to the shuttle, but unfortunately Thunderskull wasn't alone.

The deranged pirate had Two-Toe Tim's neck in one hand and an ivory-gripped revolver clutched in the other.

"Gecki, is it? And Sheni, the human?" Thunderskull was all smiles as he called out to them. "I'm not even angry that you killed my shuttle pilots and escaped. I'm impressed, really. I wish everyone on my crew was as resourceful as you two! But I can't allow you to leave with that egg. It's not the credits, you understand. It's the principle. If I let you get away with it, I'll have every two-bit spacer in the galaxy thinking they can help themselves to my hoard. When would it end, right?"

He raised the gun and pressed it against Tim's temple.

"So hand over the egg right now or I'll kill your friend."

Gecki looked across at Sheni and shrugged blankly as if to say, *Fine by me*.

"This egg doesn't belong to either of us," Sheni called out before Gecki had a chance to sign Tim's death warrant. "It belongs to the people of Keet. We need to give it back."

Thunderskull glanced at Two-Toes, then back at Sheni in confused amusement.

"You do realise I *will* blow this guy's brains out, right? This isn't a bluff. I know he was the one who unlocked the vault for you. But chuck that egg over, and both you and Toes here can walk free. Pirate's promise."

Gecki shook her head. Thunderskull was lying. Two-Toe Tim was a dead man walking. And the second they handed over the krustallos egg, their only bargaining chip, so were they.

"I've got a counter-offer," Sheni shouted. "How about you kiss my—"

And that's when the *Howling Rat's* battery tanks exploded.

CHAPTER
TWENTY-THREE

They didn't see the explosion, but they sure felt it reverberate through the hull. Sheni and Gecki were flung against their respective crates, while Alan tumbled between them like a billiard ball. Elsewhere around the helm, pirates staggered about and fell on their arses, finally looking as drunk as half of them probably were.

"Your handiwork, I assume," Gecki snarled to a dizzy Alan.

A few of the shaken pirates panicked and resumed firing at Sheni and Gecki's crates. Two-Toes had leapt off the platform during the commotion and was presently cowering behind a vat of speeder fuel. Thunderskull picked himself up, dusted off his black coat, and screamed at his crew.

"Stop shooting, you morons! The shields are down. You'll space us all!"

Sheni glanced up. Thunderskull wasn't wrong. The faint, flickering shield that protected the ship from external threats was spluttering on and off – mostly the latter. It must have drawn power from the same battery tanks that supplied juice to the ion thrusters.

"Erm, Gecki?" he asked.

"What, Sheni?"

"This dome above our heads... how tough do you reckon it is?"

"Without a shield? Probably about as tough as an antique snow globe. Why?"

"Oh, nothing." He subtly raised his eyebrows towards the rear of the ship. "But I reckon we should think about making a move..."

One of the giant charging pylons had broken free in the explosion. It spun like a majorette's baton as it drifted slowly towards the helm.

"Damn the gods," Gecki rasped, grabbing Alan and his sack of loot. "Run!"

They sprinted back towards the stairwell. A couple of pirates ignored Thunderskull's order and tried their luck at shooting the moving targets. Thunderskull roared in frustration and, without any sense of irony, shot them both in the head as punishment.

The shadow of the pylon washed over the helm...

The stairs were only a few metres away, hooded by a security station that could automatically lock shut should a depressurisation event occur. Standard issue, even on a ship like the *Howling Rat*. If they didn't make it to the door in time, or if the rapidly failing power supply caused a lockdown, they'd be stuck up there with no means of escape save for the neighbouring vacuum...

Two-Toe Tim clearly had the same idea, because he sprinted out from his hiding spot faster than Sheni reckoned any human had run before. Thunderskull spotted the traitor, raised his revolver... and then let it fall back to his side as he saw the ravaged charging pylon swing down towards the dome like a hammer wrapped in torn streamers.

Gecki chucked Alan through the opening to the stairwell just as the pylon crashed through the ceiling. Being metal, the transparent panels didn't shatter but instead buckled heavily, sometimes exposing slivers of cosmos and in other places collapsing entirely. The head of the pylon plugged some of the gap, but the change in pressure was immediate. Sheni's ears popped and his eyes watered as precious oxygen rushed out of the ship.

He felt a scaly arm wrap around his own. Squinting, he saw Gecki pulling him through the security doorway. Her teeth were bared. It was hard work, even for her. Alan hung onto a guardrail for dear life, but not even a catastrophic breach could wipe the smile from his face.

Pinning himself against the wall inside the stairwell, Sheni turned back to the helm. His eyes felt like they were being sucked out of his head, but he forced himself to search the upper deck for Two-Toes. He spotted him crawling along the floor about eight metres off to the right, in the shadow of the shipping container behind which Gecki had taken cover, pulling himself from grate to grate with an expression of sheer agony on his rippling face.

"Keep fighting, Tim," Sheni shouted over the whistling rush of air. "You can do it!"

He didn't know if Two-Toes could hear him, but the wannabe pirate appeared to gain a second wind. He dug his fingers through the slots of vents, into the shallow cracks between rusty floor panels, dragging himself forward, teeth gritted hard enough to crack.

Six metres. Five, four...

"Grab my hand," Gecki rasped, reaching out through the doorway.

The pylon groaned. Its hinged arm jutting out from the dome was still being carried forward by the residual force from the original explosion. The more it shifted, the greater the hole in the ceiling grew, and the greater the hole grew, the more the pylon shifted. Thunderskull, who remained standing at the helm in mad disbelief that this could be happening to him, on his *own ship*, stared up at the exponentially increasing breach while all around him his lackeys were gradually sucked out into the purple void.

With a sharp, metallic shriek, the pylon snapped free and tumbled into the nebula. Thunderskull activated his mag boots to keep from being dragged out with the rest of the pirates and supply crates, for all the good remaining on the upper deck would do him without a space helmet. Two-Toes screamed in pain – not that Sheni could hear him, what with the air blasting past in the opposite direction – and then lost his tenuous grip on the floor. He tumbled backward, smacked his head on the lip of a shipping container, and cartwheeled out through the jagged hole.

Gecki jerked her arm back just in time to avoid having it amputated by the security door as it slammed shut, finally cutting off the helm from the rest of the ship.

"Huh." She ran her tongue over her upper teeth. "That's a downer. Oh well."

"We have to help him," Sheni insisted, straining to pry open the door.

"He's dead." She placed a firm hand on his shoulder. "And we will be too if we don't get the hell off this ship."

Sheni looked into her cold, milky eye, nodded disappointedly, and followed her back down the corridor in the direction of the hangar. Alan tottered along behind them, still carrying his jingling sack of loot. The corridors were marginally less treacherous now that everyone else on board had bigger priorities than shooting a bunch of stowaways. The few pirates they crossed paths with barely gave them a second glance as they sprinted toward the *Howling Rat's* docking bays and lifeboats. The ship wasn't any quieter, though. New alarms blared, this time to signify a total system shutdown, and every other piece of plumbing they passed erupted from the mounting pressure. An electrical fire had broken out down one of the passageways connecting starboard and port.

The ship groaned and lurched. Sheni stumbled through a puddle below a busted pipe and wondered how long the artificial gravity system would last. He didn't fancy floating his way back to the shuttle.

"Without her thrusters, the *Howling Rat's* falling towards the vortex," Gecki explained. "It's starting to tear apart."

They arrived at the hangar thirty seconds later. The industrial blast doors were wide open. The skiff was gone. So was the two-seater speeder. If there were escape shuttles on board – Sheni wouldn't have been surprised if only one existed, and it was attached to Thunderskull's private quarters – they were surely missing, too. Only the shuttle remained, exactly where Gecki parked it.

Naturally, it exploded as the fuel pump next to it overloaded.

"Gods alive," Gecki roared as a razor-sharp shard of hull twirled over their heads and buried itself deep in the hangar wall. "Just once can the galaxy give us a freakin' break?"

"What are we going to do now?" Sheni screamed, running his hands through his hair. "The shuttle was our only way off this ship!"

"I dunno, Sheni! *You're* the one who always survives by the skin of his teeth!"

"Epithelial enamel," Alan gurgled.

"Don't start with that nonsense, Alan," Sheni replied. "We're only in this mess because of you!"

"Don't shout at him," Gecki snarled. "It's not his fault he's thick!"

"Oh, will you stop?" Thunderskull snapped.

Sheni spun around with his rifle at the ready. Thunderskull leaned against the frame of the doorway behind them, breathing heavily. His chalky, keratinous face was half covered in blood from a nasty gash across his forehead. One of his legs looked broken. Presumably his revolver had been lost in the breach, because both his hands were raised to show he was unarmed.

"The only consolation for going down with my ship," he said with a sneer, "is knowing that I'll be taking you idiots down with me. All this for an egg. Was it worth it? Knowing it'll just burn up with the rest of us?"

"It was still the right thing to do," Sheni replied, albeit without much conviction.

"The right thing?" Thunderskull laughed. "What sort of pirates are you? *Surviving* is the right thing. *Thriving*. And you can't climb to the top without stepping on those below. You humans are never gonna make it in this galaxy if you don't learn that."

The *Howling Rat* hitched violently as something else exploded. Thunderskull reached into one of his pockets. Sheni raised his rifle again, but the ship's captain only pulled out a small bottle of whiskey.

"You can shoot me if you want," Thunderskull muttered between swigs. "We share the same fate either way."

"Don't be so sure of that," Gecki rasped.

A loud, whooshing growl filled the hangar. At first, Sheni thought it was another explosion – perhaps one big enough to finally take out the spluttering forcefield protecting them from the vacuum outside. But it was just a ship swooping in to land.

Sheni laughed. Never in his life had he been so happy to see the *Silver Hart*.

Xotl waved at them through the cockpit windows as they brought the ship to a hovering stop a metre or so off the ground. The exterior airlock door hissed open. Thunderskull pulled away from his doorframe, grimacing as he put pressure on his wounded leg.

"Hey, you can't leave me here to die! Take me with you!"

"Are you kidding?" Sheni laughed incredulously. "Fat chance. You stole the egg out of our hands, you know, back when we still wanted it. You framed your heist on us."

"You wanted to sell me into slavery," Gecki snarled.

"And let's not forget the fact your crew has been trying to kill us for the past half hour," Sheni added. "Though I suppose we did blow up your ship. I guess we can let that one slide."

They clambered up into the airlock – Alan and his hessian sack first, then Sheni and Gecki. Thunderskull hobbled after them.

"I'll pay you," he yelled over the roar of the *Silver Hart's* thrusters. "Whatever you want from the vault, it's yours!"

Sheni and Gecki shared a glance, then shook their heads together.

"Sometimes, principles are worth more than credits," Sheni shouted.

"And there are some things money can't buy," Gecki added, grinning and licking her teeth.

Thunderskull threw his bottle, which smashed harmlessly against the *Silver Hart's* hull. The airlock doors locked shut just before the ship exited through the forcefield. Sheni watched Thunderskull continue to yell expletives at them through the window before collapsing to the floor as his wounded leg gave way.

With decontamination complete, Sheni and Gecki raced up to the cockpit. Xotl was frantically fiddling with a number of different dials and switches.

"Get us out of here," Gecki snarled.

"What do you think I'm trying to do?" Xotl replied. "The vortex is too strong. We don't have the acceleration to escape its pull."

"Are you saying we'll be sucked in like the *Howling Rat?*" Sheni asked.

"Unless we can increase our velocity, yes."

"You're a fool for coming to rescue us," Gecki rasped. "Now we're all going to die."

"Don't be ridiculous, Gecki. You needed my help. What else was I supposed to do?"

Sheni looked down at Alan.

"Have you got any bright ideas?"

Alan tossed his sack onto Sheni's seat and then waddled off in the direction of the engine room. Sheni took off the backpack containing the taped-up krustallos egg, shrugged desperately at Gecki, and then followed him downstairs. There wasn't anything useful he could do in the cockpit, anyway.

He shielded his face with the back of his hand. The engine room was sweltering. Xotl was already pushing the *Silver Hart* as hard as she would go. Half of the components glowed an angry red colour. The hull creaked and groaned from the strain of fighting against the purple nebula. Sheni hadn't a clue how anyone was supposed to squeeze more juice out of something already so fully pulped.

Alan approached the primary engine, his eyes swivelling between all of the injectors and crankshafts and cylinders. Sheni tapped his foot as he waited for something to happen.

"Hello? You in there, Alan? If you know a way to make this ship go faster, now's the time to do it."

Alan blew a tiny spit-bubble, raised his wrench, and then began smashing the crap out of a limiter module. Sparks erupted from the wires within.

"Stars above." Sheni backed away in horror. "What the hell are you doing?"

A high-pitched whine filled the engine room. Sheni was suddenly thrown towards the rear of the ship. He was lucky not to scald himself on any of the red-hot pipes. The engine shook like a toaster in a tumble dryer. Alan stood with a gormless smile on his face for a few seconds, blinked twice in quick succession, and then pulled a lever close to the wrecked module. The whine retreated and the engine ceased its quaking, though the limiter continued to spit out sparks.

"I don't know what you did," Gecki shouted down from the cockpit, "but it worked. Both of you, get up here."

Sheni patted Alan on the head.

"Nice one, you little maniac."

He hurried back upstairs with Alan in tow. Xotl had brought the *Silver Hart* to a safe distance from the Sydney-Wilson Vortex, then swung her around to face it. A few yellow warning lights flashed across the cockpit's dashboard thanks to Alan's improvised handiwork, yet Xotl's arms looked noticeably more relaxed than they had when Sheni first boarded.

"There she goes," Gecki snarled, crossing her arms. "Good riddance."

The *Howling Rat* drifted lifelessly into the Purple Sunset. Lightning sizzled down its length. No amount of armour plating could shield it against the gravitational might of the vortex. They watched as the ship first cracked in half, then split into increasingly smaller chunks the more the nebulous clouds embraced it.

"So much treasure," Sheni sighed. "Lost forever."

"So, what's it going to be?" Xotl asked, spinning around in their chair. "Back to Keet, or a trip to see Peggi at the Corpse & Casket?"

Gecki uncrossed her arms and growled noncommittally.

"How's our eggy friend?" she asked.

Sheni checked inside the backpack. His curiosity was met by a loud squawk. He quickly buckled the flap shut again.

"I don't think tape's gonna cut it... Alan, I don't suppose you have any glue?"

CHAPTER
TWENTY-FOUR

Gecki cursed under her breath as she descended the vertical shaft that bored through the centre of the Sunrise Temple's rock formation. The rock was damp. Gecki was a big fan of moist surfaces, but not when she was climbing. They stopped her pads from sticking properly.

The krustallos cave (as Sheni insisted on calling it) crawled with Nasakoan guards, which Gecki thought was pretty stupid. The place had been too sacred for them to enter back when the egg had actually been present. All they were doing now was making it harder to put the godsdamn thing back.

Slowly does it...

Gecki moved carefully, not only because of the possibility she might slip, but also in case anyone in the chamber below bothered to look skyward. She may have been camouflaged, but Sheni's backpack containing the krustallos wasn't. Floating bags tended to unsettle people.

And it wasn't just putting the egg back she had to worry

about. Oh, no. Then she had to escape back up the shaft without anyone noticing her, too.

Funny how this entire heist had been Sheni's idea, and yet here she was, risking her scales to put things right. He could talk about turning a new leaf and taking responsibility for his actions all he wanted, but some things never changed.

She reached the bottom of the shaft, crawled along the ceiling, and dropped quietly to the floor behind the giant, calcified krustallos. Gecki paused for a moment, making sure none of the guards could see her, and then unfastened the backpack.

The egg was stuffed inside. And the baby krustallos was inside the egg, just about. Its taaffeite shell wobbled about as the poor thing fought to break free. Gecki felt bad for it, but it wouldn't have to wait much longer. And the way she saw it, a moment of discomfort was more than worth the lifetime of worship it was about to receive. If only everyone in the galaxy could be so lucky.

She pulled it out of the bag and winced. They hadn't done the cleanest job of putting the egg back together. The duct tape was gone, at least. Most of the shards were glued roughly where they were supposed to go. Roughly. She doubted anyone except maybe the High Priest would notice, especially after it hatched, at which point everyone would have much better things to concern themselves with.

"Shhh," she whispered. "You're home now."

Gecki poked her head above the spine of the dead krustallos and checked for guards. One had wandered off down a tunnel, and the other two were talking in the corner by the trickling rock pool. She slithered out of cover and carefully nestled the egg back where they originally found it. One pat on the egg for good luck, and then Gecki scampered back up the shaft before anyone could notice her.

She was halfway up when she heard the first cry of surprise from down in the cavern. More excited yelling quickly followed.

Gecki smiled to herself, though it was a mischievous smile, and she was glad Sheni wasn't around to mock her for it.

Sure, being nice didn't pay. But she supposed it didn't cost them anything, either.

Her grin gradually morphed into a sneer as she climbed.

Well, except maybe thirty thousand credits' worth of taaffeite...

Sheni elbowed Gecki and Alan excitedly.

"Hey, quiet. It's about to start."

The three of them sat on a beam of wooden scaffolding on the far edge of the market square. They'd invited Xotl, of course, but the Xocha hadn't wanted to risk catching something. Sheni was wearing the tatty robe he stole just in case somebody in the streets recognised him. But, generally speaking, everyone was too excited by the news to care.

The krustallos egg had returned. The hatching ceremony could finally begin.

Sheni popped a handful of seeds into his mouth as three of the temple's monks hastily carried the egg onto the stage and positioned it on the cushioned plinth. Guards stood stoically between the columns and patrolled the streets surrounding the square. Not that they had any real hope of policing the crowd. The turnout was enormous, double that of when Sheni first attended the festival. Either fear of a second pirate attack didn't weigh on the Nasakoans' minds, or this once-in-a-lifetime opportunity was worth the risk. They'd emerged from their homes in droves. Travelled from neighbouring cities too, he reckoned. The yellow and purple garlands were back on display, transforming the square into a meadow of petals, and Sheni wished he and Gecki hadn't tossed theirs away before sneaking into the temple. To be even a small part of something so spectacular was quite special.

And to think they'd almost ruined it.

"Look, there's High Priest Szaladar!" he said through a mouthful of seeds.

Gecki snatched the packet out of his hand and offered some to Alan.

"Just shut up and watch," she rasped.

Szaladar marched out from one of the tunnels at the rear of the stage. His presence summoned widespread cheers from the audience. Sheni felt a pang of guilt. The past couple of days had added a decade of wrinkles to the old man's tentacled face.

He smiled and gestured for quiet. The crowd simmered down.

"Tragedy, here in Keet, has been twofold," he said, his frail voice carrying across the otherwise silent square. "First, the loss of our great krustallos, the guardian of Nasako's skies. And then, last night, the slaughter of good Keet citizens by barbarian spacers. Their deaths will live with us now, and for every Sunrise Celebration to come."

Much solemn muttering from the crowd.

"Fortunately, however," Szaladar continued, his voice brightening, "the egg the barbarians destroyed was only a replica. Many of you likely suspected this already. And as you can see, tales of the true krustallos's theft have been greatly exaggerated."

Everybody whooped and whistled. Yellow petals and purple clouds burst into the air as people tossed garlands and handfuls of dry paint. High Priest Szaladar smiled proudly at his congregation, who had weathered so much and yet still held onto hope. Sheni and Gecki looked at one another and shrugged.

"And now," the High Priest continued, "please be silent for the hatching."

He stepped aside and the crowd hushed. The egg wobbled on the cushion, tipping this way and that, but no baby broke through. Sheni sucked his teeth.

"Erm, you don't think we glued it back together *too* well, do you?"

"They've got pikes, don't they?" Gecki picked a seed out of her teeth. "I'm sure they can cut open a hole if it gets stuck."

As she said this, a segment of eggshell popped up with a snapping noise that rang out across the square like a whip crack. A collective intake of breath. A tiny reptilian head squinted towards the thousands of eyes staring directly at it and let out a curious squawk.

The city erupted. The baby krustallos, either excited by the crowd or fearful of it, fought even harder to escape its egg. Suddenly the whole shell shattered outwards. The krustallos hovered where the egg had been, batting its leathery wings heavily in the stifling evening air. Its flat tongue darted in and out. Its long, snake-like body curved and coiled into runic shapes.

"Take to your skies, Great Protector," Szaladar announced, so mesmerised that he almost forgot the ancient lines tradition required him to say. "Remind us that while the Purple Sunset may threaten our world's future, we live life to its full today."

The krustallos shot away from the temple's stage like a living arrow, zigzagging above an ocean of outstretched arms. Fireworks exploded in its wake. As the sun began to set behind their planet's young guardian, bands kicked into songs, drinks flowed, and the people of the city embraced. All was good on Nasako once more.

Gecki leaned over to Sheni.

"You know, now I think about it, a live krustallos would fetch an even higher price with some collectors than its egg..."

"Right, I think that's our cue to leave." Sheni climbed to his feet. "I don't think we'll want to stick around after the party dies down, anyway. Fingers will be pointed, you know?"

"Yeah, I dare say we won't be visiting this planet again any time soon. Come on, Alan. Don't forget your sack."

Alan hopped up beside them with a hiccup. He insisted on bringing his hessian sack of stolen treasure everywhere he went. Sheni couldn't fathom why he didn't just leave it on the ship for Xotl to look after, but the green fruitcake surely had his reasons.

"That's an awful lot of treasure you've got in there," Gecki said, as they made their way back to the *Silver Hart*. "It belongs to all of us, you know. Even split."

Alan spluttered blissfully.

"What do you want to spend it on?" Sheni asked.

"Steam baths of Haldeir-B," she replied without a moment's hesitation. "The iridium really unclogs the scales."

"I might have to pass on that," Sheni replied with a furrowed brow. "I was thinking somewhere tropical, myself.

The sort of place that does fruity drinks with little umbrellas, you know?"

"Haldeir-B has a lot of mosquitos," Gecki snarled, "and a lot of beer."

"That'll do."

They strolled into the quiet dock, the festival music reduced to a distant rumble. Another ship was parked beside the *Silver Hart*. Their faces fell as they spotted the stout, pot-bellied creature standing beside it.

"It never ends," Sheni groaned. "What the hell is *he* doing here?"

Morty Slugbarrow waddled across the dusty clearing with a grin lurking under his engorged snout. Three of his armed lackeys spread out and surrounded them.

"Is that for me?" He snatched the sack from Alan's hands. His greedy eyes bulged when he peered inside. "Early period Neceyro coins, a crown belonging to the exiled Argentan monarchy, oh, even a Trulljanan mug... Thank you very much."

"You can't take all of it," Sheni protested. "There's way more than three thousand credits in there!"

"Three and a *half* thousand credits, you owe me," Slugbarrow replied. "Plus interest, of course. And expenses, like having to fly all the way out to this dump to collect." He pulled the sack's drawstring tight. "Yes, I think this will cover everything just fine. Pleasure doing business with you. Consider yourselves off the hook."

He clicked his pudgy fingers. His lackey with the burly red backpack marched to their ship and typed in a code on the tracking device she'd installed back at the Corpse & Casket. It detached with a sound like forks being scraped along a plate and left a ring of nasty punch-holes in her tailwing.

Alan reached up for the bag with his pathetic noodle arms. Sheni reckoned it was just the moth-eaten sack he wanted returned to him. He glanced at Gecki, who shrugged lethargically. If this got Slugbarrow off their backs for good, she no longer cared.

"Don't worry, Alan," he said, guiding the poor sap away from the loan shark and towards the *Silver Hart's* airlock instead. "We'll buy you a new one."

"Burlap," he babbled mournfully. "*Crocus.*"

"That's right, man. Whatever you say."

"See you around, friends!" Slugbarrow waved them goodbye. "Next time you need credits, you know who to call. I'll give you a good rate!"

Sheni grumbled to himself as the airlock cycled through its decontamination process. Xotl eagerly waited for them on the other side.

"Is it done?" they asked. "Is it over?"

"Ship's still ours," Gecki growled irritably. "So let's use it to put a galaxy between us and that slimy parasite."

CHAPTER
TWENTY-FIVE

The *Silver Hart* lurked on the edge of Nasakoan space, its thrusters off, drifting like a stray asteroid or a piece of battlefield debris.

They hadn't got much fuel in the tanks, and they had even less idea of where to go.

"We should have fought harder to keep some of that treasure," Sheni said in the cockpit, leaning back in his chair. "Even just a few of those trinkets could have kept us going another half standard, you know? And look how sad losing that sack's made Alan."

Gecki craned her scaly neck. Alan stood in the cockpit doorway, his favourite wrench held aloft, a smile of deranged proportions etched permanently across his simple face.

"Yeah, he's devastated," she rasped. "Trust me, Sheni. It ain't worth fighting with Slugbarrow. Guy's almost as rotten as Thunderskull. Better to cut ties with him happy than give him a reason to keep following us around."

"Yeah, I guess." Sheni smiled and laced his fingers

behind his head. "And hey, we kept the ship, didn't we? Like I'm always telling ya, everything works out fine in the end."

He winked at her. Gecki bared her teeth and shook her head.

"We should decide where we're headed next," Xotl said, spinning their egg-cup chair away from all the yellow warning lights occupying the dashboard, "even if it's just a somnium depot. If anyone from Thunderskull's crew is still in the system, we're in trouble. I don't think that skiff of theirs has a skip drive, but it definitely had a turret. And even if they are gone, sooner or later a passing scrapper's going to think we're salvage."

"Any suggestions?" Gecki asked.

"A hypermarket," Xotl replied. "Our pantry is bare. Apologies. I consumed the last protein puck while you were on the *Rat*."

"How about a resort moon?" Sheni added. "They give out free drinks to card players. Maybe they'll stretch to a tray of nachos, too. And just think how much we could win on the holo-races..."

Gecki snapped her head towards him with a snarl.

"Please tell me you're kidding..."

"Of course I am," he said, reaching across the aisle to punch her on the shoulder. "Lighten up, lizard. I'm with Xotl on this one. I'll go anywhere that does half-decent grub."

"You know, you've reminded me of a rumour I heard." Gecki scratched her scales in deep thought. "Crashed casino cruiser over in the ninth quadrant. Nobody's been able to reach it for years. Millions of credits, just lying in a vault for someone to find..."

"Oh, so it's insane when *I* suggest something like that,"

Sheni replied, "but when *you* come up with a harebrained scheme to get us all killed, suddenly it's savvy, right?"

"I wasn't suggesting anything, human. Just telling you what I heard. And it's *my* ship, remember? I'm the captain. We'll go wherever I godsdamn want."

"Please stop arguing," Xotl spluttered, their arms wilting. "Our priority has to be foodstuffs. I can feel my metabolism slowing with each passing minute…"

Alan listened to everyone bicker for a little while longer, then tottered down to the engine room. It was all well and good arguing over a destination, but they wouldn't be going anywhere if the primary engine couldn't combust properly.

The broken limiter continued to spit out sparks. He waddled up to it and delicately placed his last piece of treasure where all the split wires had once joined. The tiny shard of krustallos egg glittered like silver starlight. Alan pulled the lever beside it.

Electricity crackled through the egg shell. The engine emitted a healthy rumble. Taaffeite crystal made for a fantastic conductor.

"Look at that," he heard Xotl say up in the cockpit. "All the warning lights have vanished. Either the ship's about to explode, or we're safe to fly. Dare I ask again where we wish to go?"

Alan smiled and gurgled to himself as Sheni and Gecki resumed their endless squabbling.

He didn't mind where in the galaxy they went, just so long as they all went there together.

THANK YOU FOR READING!

The adventure continues in Shadows in the Snow.

And you might want to check out The Final Dawn if you haven't already – it's the series in which Sheni and the crew of the *Silver Hart* first make an appearance.

Turn the page for a full list of titles set in the same universe as Shadows in the Stars.

BOOKS IN THE "DARK STAR PANORAMA" UNIVERSE

Final Dawn Series

- The Final Dawn
- Thief of Stars
- A Dark Horizon
- The New World
- The Tin Soldiers
- Ghost of the Father
- The Stellar Abyss
- The Edge of Night
- The Fatal Dark

War for New Terra Series

- Sigma
- Iron Nest
- Royal Blood

Shadows in the Stars Series

- Shadows in the Stars
- Shadows in the Snow

Kapamentis Crime Series

- A Cut Below
- Cut to the Bone
- Cut and Shut
- The Final Cut

Standalone Novels

- Saturnalia

SELECT NON-DSP TITLES

- Checking Out (Box Set)
- Blackwater (Box Set)
- The Portrait Lingers Like a Whisper
- Gerald Oddman

WANT A FREE, EXCLUSIVE BOOK?

Building a relationship with my readers is one of the best things about writing. Every now and then I send out newsletters with details on new releases, special offers and other bits of news relating to my books.

And if you sign up to the mailing list I'll even send you a **FREE** copy of *The Ultimate Dark Star Panorama Compendium*, an exclusive guide covering every aspect of my Dark Star Panorama universe, from a full timeline to a comprehensive encyclopaedia. It also contains *Before the Dawn*, a short prequel to my *Final Dawn* series.

Sign up today at twmashford.com.

ENJOY THIS BOOK? YOU CAN MAKE A BIG DIFFERENCE.

Reviews are the most powerful tool in my arsenal when it comes to getting attention for my books. As an indie author, I don't have quite the same financial muscle as a New York publisher. But what I *do* have is something even more effective:

A committed and loyal bunch of readers.

Honest reviews of my books help bring them to the attention of other readers.

If you've enjoyed this book I would be very grateful if you could spend just five minutes leaving a review (it can be as short as you like) on the book's Amazon page.

Thank you very much.

ABOUT THE AUTHOR

Tom Ashford lives just outside London, England with his wife Jenny and extremely needy cat, Kathleen.

An avid movie buff and video game addict, Tom loves all things science fiction. That's why he started the *Dark Star Panorama* universe – an ever-growing tapestry of epic spacefaring stories including the *Final Dawn, Kapamentis Crime* and *War for New Terra* series.

His favourite authors are Terry Pratchett and Stephen King.

facebook.com/TWMAshford
instagram.com/ashfordtom